Ghost Words and other Echoes…

Adina Pelle

Books can be ordered from Amazon.com, BN.com, other online bookstores and:

www.bytechservices.com
1500A East College Way #554
Mount Vernon, WA 98273

www.adinapelle.com

To Elizabeta

Adina Pelle was born in the ancient seaport of Constanta, where Roman poet Ovid lived his final years. Reading Ovid's *Metamorphosis* at a very early age ignited her love for the written word.

As a lonely, peculiar child, she engulfed herself in books. In an astonishing amount of reading, she experienced love and pain and kindled a desire for social justice inspired by the pages of Russian, British and French literature.

After living in many places all over the world, she moved permanently to USA in 1989. Her pilgrimage fueled a unique perception of the world.

For many years, she managed art galleries in Philadelphia, Chicago and Pittsburgh and later became a business analyst for an insurance company. As a result, when crafting her stories, she combines the dispassionate attitude of science with the sensitivity and psychological insight of an artist.

She now lives in Connecticut with her husband Stan.

ISBN 978-0975-43146-3

Published by:
Bytech Services
Curva Peligrosa Press
1500A East College Way #554
Mount Vernon, WA 98273

Author's Note

Memories form a web of shadows characterizing my *All the world's a stage* part of life.

Everyday love and the support of my husband gives my life meaning, and makes me happier than I have ever been. He helps me organize my chaotic passions.

My parents and grandparents made me everything I am. They, along with everyone else I loved in my life, helped me slip through the imaginary door between dream and reality, fly over lakes of despair and fields covered with thoughts like flowers—and snow-bound mountains representing years of relentless wandering.

The final result is my uncompromised effort to say a beautiful thing here, there and everywhere along the way.

E-mail me at adinapelle@sbcglobal.net or my publisher at kcoffman@sos.net if you have questions or comments. As always, online reviews are greatly appreciated.

For additional information, surf to www.adinapelle.com

Introduction—Imaginary Autumn

Occasionally, I feel panic while pondering my life—an unsettling anxiousness comparable to the split second after shutting a car door and seeing the keys inside. Dangling. There's no going back…the deal is done.

My life is filled with useless details and memories pushing the edge of the absurd, so I woke one morning and started a maintenance plan to put my mind in order. I recorded my recollections—memories accumulated like rusty leaves. My life and its silly twists with the many men I loved—the ones I married, the one I buried, and the lingering lessons sorted and classified as wisdom.

Some people are born with inherited astuteness about the world. Others labor for it. I am among those who work hard and suffer—carrying heartbreak and the weight of years as scars on my spirit.

When I was young, happiness meant having the energy for combat. Energy to discover life, love, pain—to fight for social justice. I fell in love, married, became a parent, got divorced—all filtered through a prism of discontent and dissatisfaction. Being an artist in a world that highly-values analytical thinking is no walk in the park; it requires navigational mastery of socio-economic order, as well as an arsenal of weapons against the mediocre and the monotonous.

Obsessively, my mind returns to this image:

The master comes home angry for whatever reason and his dog waits for him. As the scene develops, the dog jumps around—happy and wagging his tail—clearly delighted to see his master. However, the master, in a bad mood, casually kicks the dog out of his way. The poor creature whines and hides in the dark. He will never understand, and neither will his master.

The dog is lucky; he is a dog and will soon forget what happened. However, you are human and guilt leaves a stain which lingers.

So, you stare through a dirty window while the dog chases the leaves of your imaginary autumn.

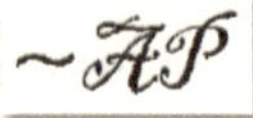

First Story

After a long hibernation in the blind spot of my mind, a story—the first story I ever knew—emerged from my psyche at unexpected times, day or night.

I will tell you, dear readers…this first story was born long ago in a faraway place at a time when I collected trinkets that made my heart smile. This was my very best little story for a long time—I loved it and it loved me. My gentle voice recounted it in front of any audience willing to listen. My family and neighborhood kids listened attentively, as if acknowledging its unhumble importance. My lovely story thought of itself as special, unique, chic and fashionable.

In reality, it was always silly, but I did not have the heart to dampen its vain spirit.

Life offered other stories along the way and I forgot about this one for a long time, but always promised…one day I would tell it to the world again and officially declare—here is my one and only first story.

In the spirit of a good first story, I should tell you how it was born, or better yet, tell you about its conception.

Have you ever thought of conception as more interesting and meaningful than birth?

Once upon a time I was a skinny and frail little girl yearning day and night for a pair of magical earrings. I saw them in my mind when I closed my eyes. They were gold or silver, long or short, with red or blue stones shimmering with facets and decomposing the sun into dazzling, broken pieces during the day—equally dancing with the moon and stars at night. I was always asleep when the moon slipped past my window and sparkled in my magic earrings, but somehow I knew.

They were charmed earrings…turning the wearer into a fairy princess. No longer drab—a princess with a cheery laugh speaking only interesting, meaningful words. Everything she touched turned into stardust.

I spun around the house wearing colored-paper make-believe earrings taped to my earlobes. Magic floated in the air.

One day my mother took me to visit neighbors—two elderly, spinster ladies who loved me dearly. While sipping lemonade and swinging my legs in the air, I noted a glass shelf suspended by silken strings.

On this shelf, sitting quietly among bottles of nail polish and perfume, sat a pair of magnificent earrings. They were the clip-on type so I would not have to pierce my ears and upset my mother. I stared at them longingly. Strands of beads that jingled when touched. In my head, the idea grew—once those earrings were suspended by my ears, a miracle would happen…people would not know me. I would tell them my name and they would not believe it. They would tell everyone they met a real princess. Starry-eyed, I looked at the glass shelf that held my magic earrings when I visited, but I never asked for them. Their secret was mine. I was sure no one else knew of the magic power locked in them.

Later, I was older and lived in a crowded city—a busy, heartless and story-less city. I forgot about the shiny magic jewels on the glass shelf. One day, I received a package from my hometown. As I opened the tiny bundle, I felt the sun entering the room. Before my eyes, sparkling red and blue, a pair of earrings worthy of a princess.

My first and most-loved story begins with a frail, dark-haired girl dreaming of magical earrings and ends with sunbeams exploding on a glass shelf in a crowded city filled with busy people who have no time for silly stories.

Adina Pelle

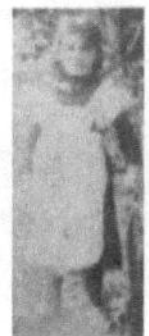

King Saul

We spend our years as a tale that is told.

"That mine adversary had written a book."
Job xxxi. 35.

In a poor but clean hut, David was born.

He was just like any other baby; no better-looking or sturdier.

After a few weeks, his small, delicate skull sprouted patches of red-gold hair, an unusual thing for his family...a genetic gift from his delicate Moabite grandmother Ruth. David was born while his parents increased and increased their brood of sons and daughters. He became the little brother, spoiled and loved without boundaries.

Delicate in flesh, but otherwise loud and stubborn—in spite of his fiery spirit he was sent to tend the goat herd.

* * * * *

King Saul was the warrior, and master.

He was dark, sturdy, capable, and brave. But robberies and attacks on his kingdom denied him peace and troubled his sleep. Far from home, David's brothers fought and defended the Promised Land from Philistines as the King asked, but their courage and mighty swords were not enough—the land fell into enemy hands.

The most-feared Philistine fighter was named Goliath; a chip from the great fighter Samson's bone. Goliath was strong and fearless.

* * * * *

When the two armies were face-to-face, a giant soldier armed with a huge mace stepped forward to face King Saul's army. He addressed them with a thunderous voice.

"You shame to yourself, Saul, for you cannot defeat me. Surrender. The war will end and we victors will take good care of your goods, women and land."

But Saul did not set his warriors against the huge Goliath. Instead the King's envoy was sent to David.

"Where is the man who wants to face Goliath?"

And David went to fight the giant.

* * * * *

The next day...

David and Goliath stood face to face. The fight did not start. Not yet. Goliath chose a spear and a gigantic, heavy sword.

David took a sling belt and a stone of suitable size, and then quietly waited for Goliath to raise his large-as-a-wagon protective shield.

* * * * *

Goliath finished his preparations and the two were face-to-face at a distance of forty feet.

Goliath looked at David.

"This is just a boy. Is this is all King Saul has left? I refuse to fight a child."

While Goliath was tensed in insult, David released the stone from the sling.

How is it possible that the giant Goliath could be felled by a stone cast by a child?

* * * * *

King Saul—freed from the giant—ruled three more years but the LORD knew he used a child to fight a monster and refused to help him further.

A messenger was sent again—this time to bring David to the palace.

As the people demanded, David was placed on the throne and Saul's body was hung outside the city wall for all to see.

His failures and sins were soon forgotten.

Don't Mind the Naked Man on the Couch—Chapter One

What if love exists only as a contortion of limbs and body heat on an old carpet? An illusion alive behind closed eyes—imprisoned by absurd prohibitions and judged harshly by a jealous world? A painful interchange of personal inadequacy buried by sordid layers of misguided truths plucked one after another and dropped like petals on an old rug splattered with indecent drops of vestal blood?

Saul's appetites and predilections devoured Matilda…a September Campaign stormed her open borders. She became his puppet state.

In shameful surrender, she built a safe, fictional world—a citadel where love's cynical incarnations lurked in corners by day—roaming free at night. With each shuddering invasion, his dark shadows consumed her.

Through it all, she never understood the beginning and end…Genesis and Revelation.

Narcissus Heart

From his days as a little boy, a very handsome man heard stories about beautiful women who stole and ravaged men's hearts. As he grew old enough to recognize love, he feared for his fate so he decided to remove his heart and hide it from the greedy eyes of women.

A witch, in exchange for a bag of gold coins, removed his heart from his chest and placed it in an ancient clay amphora—advising him to keep the light of day away from it.

He lived many years like this—without a heart in his chest or a woman to warm his nights and show him dazzling morning light pouring in from the east.

Until one day…a woman made him stop in his tracks. He turned to stare after her. She was beautiful, but many beautiful women had crossed his path before.

Were none as beautiful?

No, that was not it. This was something else. She was like a dear, sad, happy memory—a forgotten song suddenly remembered. He smiled. When the mysterious, beautiful woman smiled back, his spirit was filled with song and light.

He thought about her every waking moment. It was obvious he would need to have her around…always and in all ways.

Knowing she was poor and new to the city, he asked if she would like to share his house and life. With teary eyes, she agreed—shivering with joy.

"I am a merchant. I deal and trade, buying and selling all kinds of things in towns all over the country. Most times, I am away, but when I come home, we can spend time together. You'll be my queen and lack for nothing."

"What will I do?" she asked.

"Anything you like. Take care of the house and the pets and be yourself."

She touched his hand as a sign of agreement and leaned over to kiss him.

Days passed…the man realized his mind was less and less absorbed with trade while more and more enthralled by her crystalline voice which echoed in his mind like the clinking of magical goblets. Light followed her in stories and songs—the little things that made her happy. A colorful bird or a fresh flower filled her with the enthusiasm of a child. His eyes looked for her everywhere he traveled.

One morning his beautiful Queen embraced him and spoke with quivering voice,

"I love you." He looked at her…breathless and incapable of responding. The woman asked. "Do you not love me?"

Confused, he looked at her and replied.

"I cannot love—my heart is not in my chest."

"Where is it?

"Buried in the east wall of the house."

When he came home the next day, he found the east wall painted with beautiful flowers and birds, mountains, streams, forests and plains abounding with butterflies.

"Why did you do that?" he asked.

"So your heart is covered by my love," she said.

With embarrassment, the man confessed.

"I lied. My heart is buried at the base of the cherry tree in the garden."

"Yes?" she said with surprise.

Several weeks passed as the man went about his trade—traveling from one end of the country to the other—buying and selling nuggets of happiness to uncomplicated mortals.

When he returned, he stopped in front of the gate and stared, mesmerized, at the yard. The garden looked like a charmed ghost had breathed on it. Flowers of all colors, sizes, and smells covered the ground around the cherry tree.

"Did you do this?" he asked his queen.

"Yes," she said.

"To bring beauty and happiness to my heart?"

"Of course, that and hoping for your love to grow."

He burst out with desperation. “You should know that I will never reveal my heart—so neither you nor any other woman will steal it.”

She looked at him in shock—skeptical of his confession, before walking away without a word.

From that day on, she avoided him. No more sparkling laughter, no more songs or stories...when he traveled, he felt increasingly sad…the vacuum in his chest drained his will to face another day without her.

So, one day he secretly went home and slipped into the garden hoping to see her. To his astonishment, when he looked in the wild part of the garden, he saw her sitting by the stone that covered his mother’s grave. The urn holding his heart was buried inside that grave. She sat in the grass and sang a sad song the man had never heard before…a song that crawled deep inside his sadness. The void in his chest expanded. She looked sad and pale.

After the woman left, the heartless man walked to the tomb and desperately dug with bare hands and bleeding fingers until retrieving the amphora of his heart. With this burden, he ran to the witch who was now very, very old.

“I beg you,” he said, “to put my heart back in place so I can love. Now that I am rich, you can have as much gold as a chariot can carry. Please replace my heart.”

With her head wobbling, the witch spoke.

“I’m afraid you’re too late.”

She broke the amphora to discover the heart, the young and beautiful heart removed when he was a child, was now dry and nearly dead.

"A heart needs love to grow," the witch explained. "The only place for a heart is in the chest, where the love of your desired woman can reach it." The witch put his heart back in his chest and nursed it with incantations. "You will not live long like this. You will die little by little every day. Love can save you, but only if you return the love you receive."

The man thanked her with tears running down his cheeks for the first time since he was young. He ran home. All other things were insignificant compared to his fear of losing his heart. At home, there was no trace of his Queen. He left; giving up everything in his life, knowing this would be his last trip.

He bravely endured his journey. Sadness, laughter and crying came to him for the first time and he no longer feared for his heart. Every minute destiny allowed him was spent searching in vain for his Queen and her shimmering love.

Adina Pelle

Don't Mind the Naked Man on the Couch—Chapter Two

Waking, cottonmouthed—Matilda's mind stretched like a blanket over all memories. She tried to rise from bed but the covers were too heavy to move.

What's the rush?

Who wants to wake up anyway?

Rhetorical questions. She smiled and buried herself deeper in the sheets.

In her dream, a risqué dream if you will, all the men she ever knew were naked, and one by one, sat on her sofa.

There was Saul, dark, muscular and oblivious to his nakedness, reading the magazine she'd left on the coffee table—a woman's magazine plucked from a rack during a moment of weakness while waiting in a grocery store checkout line.

"I thought you didn't like these kind of magazines..."

Saul's voice drifted through the silence of the room. She raised her head and looked in his direction. Maybe if she said nothing about his nakedness it wouldn't be awkward.

"The fashion tips are worthwhile."

Her voice didn't seem like it belonged to her…as if heard from a distance, it was muffled and filtered.

Saul's voice was like a blunt object. A weapon.

"You never followed mainstream fashion."

"Sometimes the articles interest me."

Her voice crossed the room and returned, like an acoustic boomerang.

Saul laughed.

"You know how to perform a blow job without reading a clumsily-written article."

She should blush—it was required. She hoped she was blushing, but maybe she was too old to blush. Instead, she continued a conversation with a naked man sitting with legs crossed one on top of the other. She made a mental note. A naked man should not sit crossed-legged…under any imaginable circumstance.

"What are you doing here? Did we…"

Her sentence was terminated by more of Saul's laughter.

"We're all here, Matilda. Larry, Matt and that weird Dutch man with a name no one gets right. And, of course, young Juan you married for a day in Vegas. I am not sure who else is in the kitchen but they'll show up on the couch sooner or later."

What was this? Erotic redemption? Post-coital purgatory? Maybe last night's Vindaloo was the culprit. Everyone knows spicy food triggers hallucinations and other out-of-body experiences.

She must be dreaming, yet the naked man seemed real.

Saul selected a cigar from a wooden box on the coffee table. The cigar's smell triggered an olfactory reverie.

And, she was thirsty.

"Could I have a glass of water?" After the question left her lips, she regretted it. If Saul *was* willing to fetch her water, he'd have to get up. "Never mind, I am not so thirsty," she added quickly.

She did not want to see him standing erect.

"What do you want?" she continued. "Why are you here? Am I dying?"

She wanted to add *why are you naked* but, remembering Saul's visceral directness, was afraid of a vulgar answer.

"We're here because it's your birthday. You're not dying, but we're leaving your memory. We had our part, but now we're moving on. Larry, for example, found a nice Italian girl on the Internet. He's moving in with her."

Oh, God. Larry. I remember his Camaro with flames painted on the sides.

She tasted a hint of sourness in her mouth but hid her revulsion.

"Also, Matt's here. Older, but never married."

Matt, she recalled, was an exquisite lover. Ten years her junior, he always made her laugh. During his reign, she woke every morning with a smile on her face and a bittersweet taste in her mouth.

And Vrjen. Why does everyone struggle with his name?

She met him in Amsterdam and spent a night in his hotel bed. After too much Scotch whisky, she was left with no money, no passport, and a bellyful of anger. Her luggage, cello and wallet were stolen. The hangover lingered.

"What about you, Saul? What have you been up to?"

"Me? What do you want to hear? That I never forgot you? I did. Back in that time, I see myself moving through life as if escaping from one prison after another."

"What was to come really came—we were poisoned by our own distress," Matilda whispered.

Saul's raspy voice continued.

"Dust settled on the past, but not because I held vindictive feelings for you—it's just that dust anoints everything."

Saul spoke while Matilda hid her head under the covers.

"We lived in quiet desperation…trying too hard to find places of comfort and happiness."

Under the sheets, she nodded.

"Your problem? You looked for an impossible notion of love; something you read about or thought should be delivered by destiny."

These were Saul's final words.

She closed her eyes—hoping for the dream to change direction, but the cigar box rested on the coffee table next to the magazine and the smell of a cigar filled the air. This dream and all these thoughts were like songs of dying swans.

Her memories were finally organized.

No big, all-devouring love ever ended in a benevolent way.

Like clapping, you can only do it with two hands—an old Zen conundrum. Without two hands, there's no clapping. No stars, galaxies, or clapping hands. Whether you're a super cluster or a tiny proton, a yin or a yang…everyone and everything is hooked into everyone and everything else.

These thoughts settled in her mind. She walked to the kitchen with a clear mind and contented smile.

* * * * *

Saul was right—Matilda was uncompelled by trends. For three years in her very moist days when innocence, like cotton candy, insulated her from the scorn of the world, she lived as his clay, assuming new shapes every morning…morphing perpetually in what could be seen, in retrospect, as a blind race toward childhood's climax.

With memories awakened, she sat at the kitchen table and tried to make sense of her dream.

It's funny how life ties and unties loose ends.

"You'll always go for the dysfunctional man and this will bring shame and unhappiness on us all," her father said.

His old words lived harshly in the quiet space between wounded honor and Matilda's newfound climactic bliss. Because of Saul, Matilda grew up quickly. Her views on life, men, love, and sex were forever sealed—far from the missionary's border.

Worldly spin learned from the master. Saul had none of the pedestrian, boyish charm of other schoolboys. Instead, he had complete control to sculpt her any way he desired. She never resisted. He was her first lover—powerful, confident, old and savage. The world saw him as macabre…she followed him like a sailor follows the North Star.

Now, she could not help smiling while pouring coffee in her mug. Even in her dreams, Saul was dominant. Her history with men was guided by his will…he conducted a symphony of memories. He directed the cast of characters and arranged their subconscious stage positions.

"Lousy bastard," she mumbled, smiling.

Eventually, she wrote herself in and out of love many times—fulfilling her father's crude prophecy. She disobeyed abstract rules linked to her chastity. To her parents' horror, she married twice and walked out of life's cul-de-sacs in ill-conceived divorces.

All this time Saul was a constant in her thoughts. Like an absurd, surreal master of ceremonies, he fed her desires and fancies—showing up in her dreams every time a new lover threatened her emotional well-being. Ultimately, every man after Saul seemed no more than a prepubescent, sexually deprived victim the ogre masterfully carved into her soul.

She looked through the window—searching for a safe place to land her memories. When she met Saul, his advanced age was an issue—and made him the target of an angry world. Nobody understood how such a young girl could be content in the shadow of such a powerful, seasoned man.

"Why is she destroying her youth?" her father asked her mother.

"Why can't she go out with a nice Jewish boy?" her mother asked her father.

Matilda was her parents' only child. The youngest in her art class; she had no knowledge or experience when it came to men, sex, and love. As a blank canvas for Saul, she greedily absorbed the pleasures of the world but had no clear awareness of her place in it.

"You need to go back and learn how to be a child," Saul said while leaning over her shivering, pale body.

Every second lived in her mind…the edge of his bed, her wrinkled skirt on the floor, her pale body radiating in the dark, his eyes like beacons, green and clear, glued to the pink buttons of her breasts.

She writhed and gasped at his touch.

"I am not a child."

After so many years, her reply still echoed as an acoustic memory hidden in the secret chambers of her quirky mind.

Saul passing through made it hard to feel like a child again. A deal had to be struck with society. Her senses and awareness had to evolve. As the years passed, the echo of Saul's influence tyrannized every waking moment.

"Who's the monster that screwed you up?" Matt asked years later after touching the chill in her heart.

Between Matt's question and the next sip of coffee, Matilda reviewed random moments from her past. A forceful wind lifted dark curtains and the eternal hourglass of existence flipped over and over.

Flipping her along with it.

Don't Mind the Naked Man on the Couch—Chapter Three

Matilda finished her coffee and reached for the cigarettes she kept hidden in a drawer. Keeping them hidden was as pointless as smoking them…she stopped getting pleasure from smoking cigarettes years before. And hiding them? A *polichinelle* secret: open, yet unmentionable.

"It's my birthday," she reminded herself.

"Have a glass of port and go for a walk...think about everything your life means. Then come back and carry on."

Those were her father's words. A stoic, he never celebrated birthdays and had no tolerance for melodrama. His take on life and love was rigid and unbendable, like the stiff timbers he brought home at night when he was building their house.

He would recoil in disapproval if he knew she was seeing Saul—the thought made her raise an eyebrow. An undercurrent of submissive desire to please her father flowed in her veins, as if she was a little girl again.

Once, when she was in art school, her father paid an unannounced visit. At the time she'd moved out of the school dormitory and lived in a cheap Paris tenement patronized by ladies of the night. A large woman watched the front desk and the common baths. Her father asked the woman where the bathroom was. Her response in trashy French made Matilda laugh when she remembered the incident.

"At the end of the hall. Make sure you knock on the door. If somebody says come in—don't."

Another vivid memory: the first nude model, a man. Her jaw dropped and her cheeks turned medium Cadmium red. His perfect ensemble of bones, muscles, and radiated energy commanded her senses for some time.

"In paintings in the classical style, men are misrepresented. Michelangelo's David is perfect but with that boyish figure, he wouldn't escape unscathed from a biker bar. And what about the martyrs? Victims of religious repression wearing rags; little left of them but skin and bones."

Still in her robe...puffing her pleasureless cigarette...her thoughts drifted with the smoke in search of escape though an open window.

Saul was cynical—he smiled in condescension when she argued a point or a ventured a theory. His disregard angered her and fueled battles that stretched into the wee hours of the night.

What he never admitted was how Matilda's passion was cathartic—an aphrodisiac traveling through his blood like opium—lighting smoldering fires in the green pits of his eyes and warming his bones. They wrestled and danced the indecent, sacred, coital dance of pleasure and primitive desire after every argument.

Somehow it worked and they lived in chaotic harmony.

There is an inharmonic scale—love climbs or plummets in accordance with a sketch of melody. Matilda's many kinds of love and many ways of feeling affection traveled up and down with an imaginary score.

Her crazy eyes—eyes that cut through dreams—and her haughty, pneumatic walk were irresistible to Saul. If he was destined to live alongside one female, she was the one.

She knew he was a twisted kind of misogynist—at once likable and detestable but a perfect foil for her awakening sexuality.

And, Saul painted well. She said he painted souls.

He started with chalk on sidewalks. Orphaned at a very early age, he slept on the streets for many years. His fortunes changed when a decent couple adopted him. Once he discovered the love and comforts of home, he slept at night with ink and tubes of paint under his pillow.

Occasionally, on waking, Matilda was deeply stirred to find a new, colorful painting resting by her bed—Saul's blends of nature and sky were a joy to her eyes. And, at night, when things were good, she could hear his colors dancing between her sheets—leading to a glorious morning soaked in dewy, vibrant, multihued light.

Ghost Words

Beware of ghost words. Once voiced, they are inescapable in hospitals, monasteries, cemeteries, kitchens and wedding halls; your ears bear their racket bouncing off walls at night until they banish every good thought and feeling you ever had. Ghost words always appear at night—whispers in the dark. Often, they are mistaken words.

Of course mistaken. How could they be true? If their meanings were sincere, light would surround them—pure light and the warmth of morning.

Sometimes ghost words appear in the fading light of a gentle dusk and follow you home. They sit on the couch waiting—waiting to smother you. They creep coldly over your body and infiltrate your dreams. This is how they feed—consuming dreams. Sometimes, when they get close to your heart, they take it over and bang their fists until you lose reality's grip and sink into painful, suffocating nightmare...until you slip into unconsciousness and forget everything. Then, they eat at will, savoring your thoughts like silk worms—slippery, bitter worms on the scary edge of metamorphosis.

There are thousands of ghost words…a few hundred can take over a person, quickly growing and feeding on feelings of love, grandeur, hope and desire. Sometimes, when they overcrowd, they gather in circles and turn into tears. If they fall on the carpet, the couch or the table, they split into an infinity of meaning—forever maintaining a hold on the lost quarters of your heart.

The only enemies of ghost words are children—who audaciously kill them with spirited games. They capture the words in make-believe cages with the pure, transparent thoughts of the innocent dreamer. Ghost words back out of cozy rooms with drawings on the wall—repelled by colored pencils, plastic cars and button-eyed dolls. Adults, especially those tormented by guilt and nightmare, sleep with a teddy bear—the only true protection against sneaking, probing ghost dreams.

Their best friends are mirrors…spies of silence during the day, by night revealing images melted into the wall behind the mirror. Sometimes their agenda and entertainment create misleading, prosperous atmospheres—people do not realize how much the late night reflection is a poor projection of what occurred during the day. Deceptive and hard to believe—you know this if you pay attention—ghost words lounge in unison with perceived truth, giving birth to false rejoicing, to later strip you of all wholesome feeling.

Ladies, be careful. Hordes of ghost words can overwhelm your heart; tear it and project lurid red tint into the mirrors you find reliable during the day. The first sign of ownership appears on the lips, and then spreads to the neck and breasts. Finally the whole body is bruised by an invisible ache. The ache might bypass you, but ghost words go on to survive under the skin, night-feeding on your dreams and feelings and overloading your mind with dread.

Gentlemen, scratches on your back are the clearest signs of control. They steal your wishes. Ideas get buried under your coat for later consumption.

Beware. Ghost words are dishonest. When they possess you, in the morning you feel unearned fatigue and irrational fear.

Then, the image the mirror reflects in the morning is only a shadow wearing monochromatic pajamas.

What is the art of living? Can we experience joy and happiness while living a regular life? I see happiness as a relative notion that depends on your personal philosophy. The classic cliché: is the water glass half full or half empty? My father always said his glass was never big enough.

As I witnessed a dear friend's encounter with illness, I realized there are only two things that traverse and resonate through time and age:

Love and death.

I oscillate between focusing on one or the other. Depending on how far I am from the beginning of everything, one prevails over the other and creates an intricate labyrinth of memories…and my emergent stories.

As a Dying Man Thinketh

When I first knew him, a tsunami of chemicals bonded us. Cocaine and opiates—and the sound they made while slamming the translucent walls of our veins—framed the muddle of our youth. Our bloody vices filled the crystal goblet of our lives—a transparent receptacle held to the light by self-appointed arbitrators—judges, juries and executioners.

Ultimately I reassembled myself, recomposed my lost brokenness and saved myself from our vortex of vices and conspiracies.

When he took his turn to rise to the surface it was too late...his brain projected nightmares into MRI images and his morality tale changed from farce to tragedy.

I wasn't sure if visiting him in the hospital would be a good thing, but I went anyway.

His section of the hospital was on the top floor of the building, but unlike other patients, he was not in his bed courting pity. I was determined to find him. The hatch leading to the roof was open. I climbed the narrow steps and found him on the roof in his wheelchair—connected to an infusion bag and staring down at the city. He must have heard my steps but did not turn his head. I stood near his shoulder.

"How did you manage to get up here?"

"I'm sick, not crippled," he answered as if responding to insult. After several seconds of silence, he raised his eyes and smiled. "Are you going to sit down?"

He pointed his finger toward a collapsed wheelchair. I thanked him and sat.

"How's the treatment going?"

He answered this question all day long and it gave him no pleasure to face it again, but he was gracious.

"To hell with my treatment. My guts are tangled in a ball, my head looks like a piñata and every night I have seizures as if I'm plugged into an electric socket. Should I go on?"

He liked being sarcastic, especially when it came to his illness—it was his way of being superior to the disease that tyrannized him. It was clear he wanted to avoid other trite questions like *How are you?*, *What do the doctors say?*, and *How's your family handling everything?*

He forged ahead.

"Work is shitty, right?" He looked at my cheap, wrinkled suit and loose tie around my neck.

"I should take sick leave."

He laughed. There were few who would make jokes with him during these trying times.

We watched the city lights and enjoyed the peace.

I did not want to kill the pleasant mood with small talk. We sat in silence.

He removed a cigarette from his robe pocket, lit it, and then gestured with the package and his lighter. I took them.

"I don't know if cigarettes are the best choice for you now."

"Pfft...I might get cancer?"

"No, but they might disturb your treatment, you know."

"There's no connection. First of all, I do not have lung cancer, though I smoked for fourteen years. The problem is in my brain. I avoided thinking too hard all my life, and now I get brain cancer. Funny, no?" He took a drag from his cigarette and released smoke through his nose. "My chances are zero. Treatment will only delay the inevitable. I will die soon—final phase. A man in a relationship with death goes through four phases. First is denial, where you laugh at the doctors' predictions and affect a cool, poised attitude. The second phase is anger when you smack the doctor in the face and break something on your way out of his office because he told you there's nothing that can be done. The third is sorrow where you desperately plead with God. The last stage is depression."

"Isn't the last stage acceptance? Oneness with the universe?"

"Look, you made me sad. Let me adjust the morphine drip—maybe I'll cheer up a little." He increased the infusion and smiled with pleasure as the dose entered his body. He continued. "You know what was the best choice of my life?"

"What?"

"The fact that I did not make a choice."

"You chose to marry. You chose to have children."

"You're wrong. I was always adrift." He was pensive because of the morphine or maybe there was more to it than that. "You didn't let yourself be carried away by the wind," he said while looking into space.

"How do you know?"

He looked my way.

"Because you're here, broke and tired, and wearing an uncomfortable suit. If you made better choices, you could have been more. You have great potential, but you wasted it by being rational."

"How else would I make decisions? Guesswork?"

"No, by choosing the truth and following where ever it led. That's the only selection that counts."

"What's the truth?"

"Instinct. Choosing a path without fear because your heart sent the message in some secret Morse code."

The inapt metaphor made me smile but I let him continue because I liked seeing him in such a poetic mood.

“You think I chose to marry Ana? Do you think I analyzed my financial possibilities? Did I stand pensively asking the sky if I loved her? Fuck! I proposed the instant my soul sensed the rightness of it.”

“That was a happy day. But in life, you can’t do what you feel all the time. Maybe you want to get drunk at work, curse in a library or run naked down the street.”

“Why not? You’ll suffer consequences, but you’ll be well ahead of the game.”

“If they put you in jail for indecent exposure, it’s worth it because you indulged in a moment of madness?”

“Of course. When the cops pick you up—there’s a unique beauty in the situation. If you follow your instincts and run, you’ll have even more satisfaction. Then, in the cell, instinct might tell you to pick a fight to complete the circle of instinctual existence. Enjoy the moment. Then, life is a fulfillment of your current desires leaving no time for regrets or analysis.”

“Carpe diem?”

“No, not only live this moment, but also live each and every moment. I remember,” he continued, “the first time I acted based solely on instinct. I had a few days where I did a lot of shit and ended up with a death threat from the bunch of losers I was hanging out with. I was chased through dark alleys with by creeps with baseball bats because I stole one of the bikers’ girls. All ended well. I married the woman and spent three days and three nights with her. After that, I took off one morning when everyone was dead drunk. I never saw any of them again."

"And your wife?"

"The biker woman? You think we did a wedding with papers? They live by their law. You think they live by instinct, but not really. For example, the woman thought she had a choice whether to marry me or not, but the decision was made by the gang."

I laughed with relish. He was happy because he demonstrated theory through experience.

"And the other choices, why were they not as dangerous?"

"Many were dangerous, but you see, even instinct learns from mistakes."

I was mesmerized by how much he invested in his theory—his linear philosophy. He knew I was unconvinced, so he tried one last argument.

"Let me give you another example. Get up and stand next to me."

I did. My back was toward the edge of the building. I faced his wheelchair. He jumped up and pushed me over the edge. He caught my ankles at the last instant and held my feet while I dangled over the street twenty stories below…hanging above the abyss. Between death and me were his strong hands and weight-toned arms holding my ankles.

"Pull me back, idiot!"

"See? If you acted on instinct, you'd've grabbed me—forcing me to pull you back or go down with you. Instead you left me in control. I can drop you at any time. You realize what this means?"

"Yes, I get it, pull me the hell back."

"Your life is in the hands of a terminal cancer patient on drugs. Strong, but dying."

His eyes shone with crazy light; the mad flicker made me think I was already dead.

I didn't pay attention to details but later I realized he used up all his strength to hold me. His hands were like steel. The only way I could fall was to take him with me.

"Someone puts a gun to your temple," he continued. "What can you do? Wait to be shot? No, you elbow him in the stomach. That's your instinct. What about now? What do you do when a mad man holds you by your ankles over the edge of a twenty-story building? What do you do?"

"Count on your instincts."

"Bravo."

In that moment he pulled me closer to the edge so I could get a hold and regain the roof. He was ecstatic. I would have smacked his head but I realized he was no longer himself—he was a man scared to death of death. My heart throbbed in my chest. He pulled a spare infusion needle from his robe pocket. His smile was saintly.

"Want to share the drip and calm down?"

Like old times.

I sat back in the wheelchair and tapped his morphine bag. Just a taste, not a full dose. My body remembered chemical bliss—nearly as good as the real thing. For the rest of the endless evening we wove patchwork stories from the threads of memory until it was long past the time I needed to go home.

I got the call from his wife the next day. Overnight, he died in his sleep.

The Mutt

Late last night, as I started my walk, the cold was as sharp as a blade—a blade keen enough to cut a stone heart, even one carved from the coldest marble.

An approaching man looked a sleepwalker; shivering and bundled like a mummy. His hat was pulled over his forehead, covering his ears. A scarf wrapped around his neck covered most of his face. His coat's ragged collar bore tufts of fur like sad memories of long-departed grandeur.

He walked with his arm at an angle to his body, gripping the leash of a hidden dog—a clever dog avoiding bitter wind in his muzzle by walking behind his master.

Smart dog.

Inside, I smiled.

The brutal whip of frozen air propelled me up, down, left and right in a deranged dance I could not control. I must have looked like a mental patient but my appearance was irrelevant. I stared at the enigmatic vagabond—my fascination crossed the freezing boundaries of common sense.

He wobbled across the sidewalk as if looking for something lost. Mocking the unfortunate is unkind, but his walk amused me. His limp was pronounced. He walked as if his steps would leave deep footprints in the asphalt.

He stopped and looked in my direction…his cough sounded like a steam engine an imaginary locomotive engineer desperately tried to ignite.

Smoker.

With consumption lingering in his lungs?

With unreasonable longing, I was curious to see the hidden dog. Cold air and blown snow teased tears from my eyes.

What a night. How stupid not to be home. How idiotic to obsess over a drifter.

I warmed my hands with exhaled air and rubbed them against each other while waiting for the dog to show himself. I could not think past the dog. He must have been cold, no matter how furry he was.

We passed through a dark patch between streetlights. I squinted. The man's staggering silhouette approached—slower and slower.

Was he afraid of me?

I was spooked. My hand clenched keys in my pocket—ready for use as weapons if necessary.

I waited for the dog to prance before my eyes as if part of a military parade. My heart was heavy with pity for the sorry beast—I reserved only a fraction of my sympathy for his freakish master.

Why drag a dog out in this cold—in the middle of the night?

He'd be better off anywhere else. Like the old and decrepit, dogs should sleep in front of a fire at night.

They were close. Behind the hobo, I saw the leash streaming from his hand and hidden behind him. I imagined stifled, suffering sounds.

Poor animal.

Only a few steps away—I was devoured by curiosity, but I did not want to betray any interest in the odd couple. With eye contact would come the cadge…money for cigarettes or a bowl of soup. He dropped something.

I held my breath…I did not know whether he noticed me—he appeared oblivious to our time and place. Tracking his meander across the sidewalk, I studied the leash. He jerked the strap as if pulling a reluctant cur, but the leash terminated in thin air.

"Here, puppy-puppy," he whispered.

The late hour played tricks and my mind relaxed its hold of reality. While passing, he shook the leash as if urging the invisible dog to move along faster. The lonely leash dragged on the sidewalk.

A few steps farther, the object he dropped gleamed—a pale hint on the sidewalk. I looked to make sure they were gone before leaning over to look.

A crescent of bone glowing in dim light like a harvest moon shining through clouds. A fleshless, dead thing—pocked by the unmistakable teeth marks of an invisible dog.

Memories—the relics of experience—are the only things wholly owned by the individual. Some rely on them for survival. Others smother them with nostalgic paint covering indelible scars.

Many worship their memories and build an elaborate temple to hold them—a mental Parthenon with Doric memoirs for columns. Some souls are restless and seek a balanced spirit…soft cushions of memories sheltering consciousness—shielding veils that hide perception's tender face.

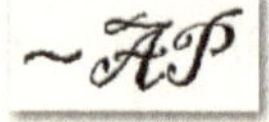

Ellie Tsar

Though retired from nursing, Ellie Tsar was passionate in her uncurbed dedication—like color and paintbrush to a painter or the written word for a writer. To her, the sick man and his suffering were basic materials from which she sculpted her life for more than forty-five years.

Every working day for almost half a century, her steps led down a sidewalk to the hospital. Saint Loup's National Hospital for Nervous Diseases…National as the locals knew it, was a red brick building surrounded by tall fir trees. Its architecture was cobbled together; asymmetrical, as if overwhelmed by amalgams of the distorted thoughts assembled within its walls.

Ellie, the central figure of this chronicle, was a tiny person with frost-white hair betraying her age. Her bare hands, gathered in her lap as if praising a deity known only to her, signified sacred dedication and sense of calm. Her voice was always full of affection and formal cordiality.

Never dressed to distract—always sober and orderly—her clothes were carefully ironed and crisp with starch. Ellie Tsar's body was always encased in black. Pants, blouse and shoes—finished with a red vest.

Her living room had the unmistakable smell of history…old books and spices. Paperback-crowded shelves—a vast collection of books laying down intellectual fingerprints.

I read them all. Proust, Dumas, Balzac, Dostoyevsky and many others gave me company all these lonely years.

She stared into space with coal-colored eyes.

What is more difficult than working with people who create their own reality?

A rhetorical question to be answered only with nodding acceptance. Ellie's story rolled like a 1920's film, but with sound, life, and truth. Her life was real.

The pages of her story started with a cliché.

Once upon a time.

I started working at the psychiatric hospital in 1963. No one should have to work in such a place. Each patient affects you. All had families—relatives who loved them—and friends who suffered for them.

Our retired nurse related events with passion, as if living each moment over again. Her job was to make sure everyone received daily medication—the proper pills and doses. She helped when a patient had an existential crisis. With some who suffered various smaller syndromes, she shared long conversations about anything and everything—fully aware the talks helped, at least briefly.

There were difficult cases...patients who were nothing but frustration.

Old memories decorated with tears.

Ellie Tsar talked about people—patients who disturbed the patterns of her thinking. Painful reflections of a life, imbued with heavy questions, mostly unanswered.

She remembered a young woman with an enviable intellect. She'd entered college with the promise of extraordinary great success, but suffered an awful disease. Schizophrenia. Her symptoms progressed quickly…everyone worried over her. In a final stage, the young woman refused food and shelter. The hand that wrote her destiny stopped and cast her soul into forever.

While remembering this sad story, Ellie rose from the couch and walked across the room. Through the window, she gazed into the sky, as if hoping for all recollection to be erased. *Useless.* A tear freed itself and trickled down her cheek.

She believed all the people in the psychiatric ward were chosen by God to suffer and thus ultimately be saved. After all, in antiquity, epilepsy patients were thought to be messengers of the gods. Her fascination with God and His involvement in all human affairs gave her an austere, stoic manner.

A weak smile adorned her face at the thought of another, happier story. Thirty years prior, a nineteen-year-old young man—Felix—walked through the front doors. He also suffered dreadful schizophrenia with similar emotional outbursts and the erratic symptoms of conscious and unconscious martyrdom.

A young person who had known the burden of disease for a long time...he very much liked to paint strange paintings—macabre, but interesting visual representations of what he felt inside.

She turned away from the window. On a table was a paper-wrapped bundle. Inside, a portrait Felix created before slipping into God's endless sleep.

The painting overwhelmed and silenced whispering voices. Like a surreal Dali dream, the canvas exposed a man on his knees with wounded hands reaching to an unforgiving sky.

If he had not died so young, he surely would have been famous.

A sad revelation from her dictionary of memories. To her left, the wall was covered with black-and-white photographs. Each had something to say—characters who spoke only to Ellie, the woman who knew them better than anyone.

Dr. Twickenham—for so many years a good friend.

Jasper, the janitor, with charcoal-smudged cheeks and Vandyck beard stained yellow from hand-rolled cigarettes.

Mrs. d'Combray who donated quilts at Christmas.

She drifted through all life's stages, ages and phases. Twenty years old, thirty years old—ascending to the present with all evolved disappointments and regrets.

How beautiful it all was...

She never acknowledged the passing of time.

…yesterday when I started at the hospital.

Yesterday, today and tomorrow—a sequence of film images thrown to the floor by a malfunctioning movie projector; disappointing an imaginary public.

In silence, the conversation ended, leaving only echoes in the great chambers of her soul.

My job was my most valuable treasure. Over the years, thousands of people in my care. Given it all to do over—again, a nurse I would be.

People are people. The angles and vectors of their lives can be determined by a guiding, helping hand when in need—providing overwhelming validation of a life dedicated to humanity.

Years ago, middle age settled over me. I had no energy to go on—I was immersed in the multimedia distractions of blog, iPod, computer, twenty-four-hour news, and credit card debt. I hardly noticed the inexorable passing of time.

I became confused about who I really was and what my life was meant to be; I lost the concept of happiness—while living in quiet desperation and trying to escape the black shroud of loneliness that descended when the sun went down. I was at my lowest point—trying to pick myself up after a failed marriage, changing jobs and raising a teenager on my own. I wondered if there was any hope of escape or if I was where I was meant to be, forever.

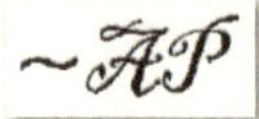

Prisoner

Sitting with my back supported by a cold, wet wall, I expected it to feel coarse, but my palms slipped along its surface and discovered only damp, worn edges.

I closed my eyes in trying to adjust to the failing light.

If I could figure out where I am, I could understand how I ended up here.

From somewhere above came a wan light, creating a faint halo in the gloom.

I sensed a deep pit like a well in a nomad castle, an *oubliette* of the sad tales where offenders and undesirables were thrown and forgotten. A summary prison—an inexorable terminus and destiny for anonymous and revolutionary alike.

What was my crime?

I tried to remember, but failed.

The external gloom matched the internal—the darkness deep inside was all the more frightening because I could not look inside and discover my identity.

I rose slowly; afraid I would feel pain from wounds of the flesh—dislocated limbs or broken ribs. Amazingly, everything was in place and undamaged. I felt no pain, hunger, or thirst. My drama did not include anything physical.

While stepping with care, I moved to the right while keeping my hand in constant contact with the wall. The floor, though wet, was clean. My outstretched arm encountered nothing but a flat stone.

Nothing seemed real.

Am I real?

With my back to the wall, I stretched my hands into space. After gathering courage, I took a cautious step—then another. After ten steps, my questing fingers encountered a wall. My eyes adapted to the faint light and I could see the extent of my confine.

Walking in circles was pointless in this square cell, so I sat down.

* * * * *

There was something strange about this room…a medieval castle's dungeon chamber should not be so clean. Self-awareness kindled in me like a campfire. I was fully dressed; I recognized the familiar coziness of my old, broken-in jeans. Jeans with a belt. A belt that should carry my cell phone's case. The case was there, but empty. Patting pockets, I discovered other deficiencies—my pockets were empty. Everything that might link me to life was missing. And yet I recognized pants, sweater, shoes and belt. I felt the elastic captivity of panties and the binding embrace of my brassiere. If this was hallucination, it was detailed enough to include the weight of eyeglasses on my nose.

In a leap of faith, I felt my confinement was intentional and happened for a reason.

Should I see God's guidance in any and every gesture?

Every event is a link between past and future, a smooth hook of yesterday's yarn into today's fabric stitched into tomorrow. Elegantly passing through this moment—the present instant hanging like a crystal, transparent drop of cold dew. My reflection was distorted in the strange shape of the liquid lens, acting as a filter of introspection.

My presence must be meaningful, even if I could not comprehend it while sitting in the evolving dark.

Was I a monk assigned the pious reflection of solitude?

To reflect on what? Any holy or divine breakthrough would split a second like an atom, converting potential energy into kinetic, producing a light revealing all.

In view of my lost paralysis—as an apparent prisoner in a pit of lost time, what purpose did my thoughts hold? If I thought of veiled monks in meditation, was it a hint I should follow suit? What else could I do while trapped in this mystery?

Eyes open or closed? Standing or sitting? Thinking of what? The worthless things missing from my pockets or the essence of divinity and my sense of life? If I had the cell phone, the display could make light. Would it matter? The darkness of my soul would absorb that light. All the light in the world would be useless if my soul was in shadow.

All the things I miss are physical and unrelated to the inner me. No identification will answer the question…who am I? Passport, driver's license and library card are fine silver chains connected to the world. Credit cards bind you to the bank, obligation and work. The driver's license links you to the car, road and state. And so on. Valueless on a desert island, for example. At the bottom of a shaft? Less than immaterial. Money? Irrelevant. Keys? See me smile. The only thing with value would be music. Could I put on headphones and listen to a song or two? A sonata. A cantata. A fugue. A madrigal.

My soul for a toccata.

And then? After a brief reprieve from the imperative?

Answers? Are they so important?

Would I sit as well if I did not care who I was and what I was doing? Maybe I was born here and this deep pit was always my home and the light above was, is and always will be incomprehensible.

With everything starting and ending in obscurity. Maybe no record of our thoughts or deeds will persist.

No. I refuse to accept it. What would life be?

We are Icarus butterflies, seeking light on our journey to perdition. We'd dissolve in a cataclysmic orgasm if we reached our ideals—they'd be too hot and too bright for us. Peace on earth, perpetual happiness, harmony with nature and, through it, the divine.

Once, I read on a forum how people struggled to beat boredom. And here I sat, alone at the bottom of a shaft, in the dark, with nothing but the clothes on my back and I was not bored.

What's more important: what is inside or outside? Which form of darkness bothers me more? If you could light your inner self, would that light be visible to others?

Light up your inner soul…where's the switch? Imagine a neophyte monk's manual…to turn on the interior light, flip the switch by the door. Which door? See page 101 of the hundred-page manual.

I concentrated as hard as I could and focused on the dark sphere in the center of my being. Fear's shadow ran through my thoughts.

The result of meditation and introspection might be shocking.

We'd be shaken and disgusted by a critical examination of the small details of our life.

Things done at certain times…maybe they were inevitable or true to the moment, but when reconsidered with cold logic—are layered with regret. Daggers stabbing the heart. Regret can grow like yanked weeds that come back with renewed force each spring.

Could the hard, square edges of my life have been avoided and replaced with doses of bliss?

There's innocence in self-abandonment. I felt a state of semiconscious ecstasy wrapping around me like a sweet cloak. Seductive, like a lover wrapping his arms around my waist—nibbling my ear and whispering.

"Stay. Don't leave."

His warm body pressed against my back; his heart beating like a distant echo.

"Does he really want me to stay?"

In staying, would I serve an animal's whim or sate a deep, true thirst for my being?

Did I want to know the answer?

If we stood before a door hiding the cruel realities of ultimate truth—a door that said: "Once through you'll find the truth about God." Would we reach for the knob or draw back? What other fundamental questions might we ask?

Are we alone in the cosmos?

If this pit was my only universe, would I find the loneliness and uncertainty of my life bearable? I am sensual, inquisitive and passionate; greedy to absorb the pleasures of the world like a starving baby attached to the maternal breast. An innocent, abandoned baby in the dark…suspended in time with a cluster of thoughts only a germ in my mind.

Am I a soul cleansed of previous existence and ready for rebirth?

The wall of my imaginary prison palpitated in synchronicity with my heart. A mysterious force ranged in my life, interpreting it for better or worse like an unseen conductor waving an imaginary baton and reading invisible music.

I felt as if I was failing this strange test, but I needed to know, so I opened my eyes.

On the wall, written in white light, was a single word.

Believe

I walked to the wall and touched the word. The paint was fresh and stained my fingers. A stepladder leaned against the wall.

Was it always there?

I was comfortable in my prison—as if I'd earned punishment and was meant to suffer, but I climbed. Tears filled my eyes. Little by little, the lip above the pit approached. I realized I was both prison guard and prisoner. Everything I ever needed was within.

One step remained; I felt victorious over fear. I'd been told over and over in action and in words: it was my place to be locked away from joy. I bore the stain of guilt and earned every penalty. I was meant to suffer and once free, would have to forever abandon my quiet, mysterious paradise.

The choice was mine.

The Icarus butterfly is an odd creature—sometimes one escapes the cruel grip of sin's gravity and reaches the sun.

When I started drafting my stories, I thought mainly of my family. My grandparents watch over me from a corner of my consciousness. Now they belong to time and history but their voices are still vivid in my mind—their story lives in me and belongs to my children and my children's children.

When I was a child, my grandfather humored my fantasies. He loved to see my eyes get wider as he told me story after story…where I came from and of people far and away. I had to imagine and attach faces—they were hidden far back in the clouds of time—there was barely any proof of their vibrant history and era.

The other day, my husband surprised me with a framed picture of my grandmother and her family. It hangs on the wall in front of me—every time my eye wanders about the room, I'm pierced by the stoic look of my family and bygone times. The snapshot is circa 1915 and was taken in the Ukraine of my grandmother's youth. She must have been around ten when the shutter snapped shut on the image. This frozen moment charges my thoughts—past, present and future. I see a reflection in the pool of my existence and my dreams fly high—then my pen seeks a clean sheet of paper.

A life's story is ready for birth.

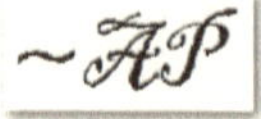

Guardian Angel

My dreams, thoughts and memories make me individual…my story overflows with joy, pain, love and loss. There are verified facts in my account—and loose ends to reconcile with reality.

Both sets of my grandparents came from faraway lands…carried by the waves of history that rocked Europe from the beginning of the 20th century through the Second World War and beyond. Borders were alive and changed from one day to the next—one could be a citizen of one country one day and bear the oppression of a different fatherland's administration in the next.

My father's father was born in Lvov—part of southeastern Poland when he was born, then occupied by the Soviet Union in 1939 under the terms of the German-Soviet Pact.

My grandmother was born in Kiev and became an orphan shortly after her family portrait was taken—the image used for this book's cover. She is the happy ten-year-old on the left side—you'll note her ghostly image used as a header for my stories.

I do not have the whole story of how my grandfather's path crossed my grandmother's. I imagined details with thoughts overflowing with potent romanticism. I'm sure the reality was simple.

Like many things: simple, but not easy.

According to family history, my grandfather saw my grandmother on the streets of Kiev and followed her home. She was an orphan adopted into her uncle's family. Her uncle and adopted family wanted to get her out of their household without expense. In those times, a girl's dowry was the most important detail for arranging a good marriage and comfortable life—the head-of-household had full authority over her future.

I tried to pull facts from my grandmother—I remember asking if she was in love with her future husband.

"What's love got to do with it?" she said.

After their marriage, they proceeded with the business of producing four children—two boys and two girls. My father is the youngest.

By 1943 my grandfather was a well-established intellectual—managing his considerable estate, which included horses, large houses and servants.

One night, he was awakened by a loud pounding on his bedroom window. A neighbor, gasping for air, whispered the news. In the morning, transport to the Gulag was scheduled and my grandfather and his family were on the list. My grandmother rose—together they roused their children. The kids ranged from three to ten—sleepy and oblivious to the tragedy in the making. With only the clothes on their backs, they left their lives of abundance, love, and happiness to embark on a journey into the unknown.

The neighbor who woke them was a poor, just-married Jewish man who knew he'd be on the first convoy for Siberia. He and his young bride joined my grandmother and grandfather in their flight into the night.

How full of surprises is life? How rich can one be owning only a change of clothes—alive only because of the warm hearts and kindness of strangers?

* * * * *

When my grandfather heard tapping on his window in the middle of the night, he knew the dark hand of the Russian revolution reached for him and his family.

Following the death of Lenin in 1924, Stalin prevailed over Trotsky—taking control of the Communist Party and imposing his reign of terror against Jews, intellectuals and the remaining landowners who survived the Bolshevik revolution. Lenin protected Jews. His speeches, left for posterity, clearly iterate tolerance towards this large segment of the Russian population.

Breaking the Nazi/Soviet alliance, German troops invaded Soviet territory in June 1941. In an odd twist, Joseph Stalin became our ally—opposing Nazi Germany and its Axis. During the summer and autumn of 1941, German troops advanced deep into the Soviet Union, but stiffening Red Army resistance prevented the Germans from capturing the key cities of Leningrad and Moscow. On December 6, 1941, Soviet troops launched a counteroffensive that drove German forces from the outskirts of Moscow.

Kiev prepared for attack. 200,000 people helped the army with preparations. On July 11th, 1941, German troops appeared on the Irpen River Bridge.

In the background of war, Stalin eliminated enemies of the revolution—sending men to the front and children and women to work camps far away on the frozen tundra of Siberia. Many families perished. These were things my grandfather knew when waking to the frantic rapping on the window.

They loaded the sleeping children on a horse-drawn cart and drove to the train station. The Jewish neighbor who woke them brought his wife along—knowing the grim fate waiting if they did not also flee.

At the train station they found the last civilian train; my grandfather had to leave his beloved horses and herd his family on. I was told how he peered into his horse's eyes before abandoning them on the station platform. This was the first rip in his heart and the beginning of a long stream of tears life would extract. My grandmother remembers him crying like a child for the first and last time in his life.

The front line moved quickly toward Kiev. Their ride was cut short when they came under air raid. Everyone had to leave the train and set out on foot. No one knew the exact situation. Rumor said the Red Cross had a refugee camp on the other side of the belt of fire. This nugget of hope motivated the four adults and four children to run through fire and mud—darkness blemished with the sparkle of demonic fire. My grandmother held my father in her arms while his four-year-old sister Galia held her hand. My grandfather, ahead, cleared a path in that inferno. The neighbor and his wife took care of the other two children—my uncle (the oldest) and my six-year-old aunt.

In a split second, my grandmother lost her grip on Galia's hand. A bright ball of fire separated them. Details are scarce, but the little girl perished that night. My grandmother watched, horrified and helpless, as her little girl perished in a mortar shell's hellfire.

What motivates people to survive grim strikes of misfortune and tragedy?

Though only three, my father remembers the run through fire and explosions.

How many three-year-olds have seen the devil's flames?

My grandmother lost her hearing—because of the explosion or the trauma of losing her child? She rarely talked about it, but never forgave herself for letting go of her little girl's hand. The only times this tough woman permitted herself to shed a tear were when immersed in these memories…

Life would be so different if things happened in an alternate sequence.

For the rest of her life, my grandmother was convinced Galia was a guardian angel watching over our family. Nobody had the heart to deny this wisp of magic dust that protected the living and commemorated the dead.

At the refugee camp, it was not a time for words or tears. It was a time for developing the stoic endurance that defined their later lives.

Kiev witnessed two battles, one for defense and other for liberation. Both were some of the biggest battles of WW2, and touched my family in ways hard to comprehend while I hunch over the glaring screen of my computer.

The Red Cross took care of the wounded, gave shelter and water to the refugees, and sorted through piles of paperwork. Some, beyond being confused, wounded, scared and traumatized, had no identification. Some feared what the future might bring if they identified themselves.

As things were unrevealed later, the young Jewish man was loaded on a Red Army transport destined for the Front. His wife was put on a different train and sent to a remote corner of Romania—she later discovered she was pregnant.

For months, alone in a strange country, she knew nothing about her husband and grew bigger and bigger with child…my mother.

After months of fighting in dismal conditions with no boots and little food and water, her husband escaped from the Reds. Maybe he deserted, maybe he was sent away. By foot, he started a journey toward Romania. Educated as an accountant, he found work as a clerk here and there, which gave him access to census records. Thus, he found his wife and arrived in her village a day before their child, my mother, was born.

After the birth, my grandparents found employment as clerks in Ploiesti where they lived for the rest of their lives.

My family's story as I heard and imagined it weaves forward through many years and many lands—tossed by the turmoil of history. They lived through defeat and rebirth; as targets, they dodged shots aimed at them. The serendipity that followed was the biggest surprise.

Two branches of my family shared a common theme—crossing the front line and filtering through the Red Cross camp, going separate ways and living full lives unaware of how destiny would bring them face-to-face again. My mother's father, while working as an accounting clerk in a census office, came across very familiar names. He wrote a letter.

My father's father and his family were settled in new lives as refugees, but never forgot the night when, in the flames and smoke of war, their lives changed with a knocking at their bedroom window.

Their children, immersed in the fabric of life, grew up, went to school and married. Then one day a letter arrived—resurrecting old memories. After twenty-five years, the Jewish man who steered their fate found them and was ready to visit.

Destiny unfolded—two young people were introduced—my father and the young daughter of the man who twenty-five years prior saved his family from perishing in the tundra and held his little hand while crossing the boundary between worlds. The fate of these families was resealed, this time under a clear blue sky with tears of joy and unexpected wonder.

Five months later my mother and father were married and I was conceived.

The two families never separated again and I entered this world under the loving gaze of the most loving pair of grandparents any little girl would wish for.

Guided and protected by our guardian angel.

My grandmother told me this story—her brother ended up in Siberia when Khrushchev deported nearly an entire generation of university students perceived as *enemies of the people*. After years of labor in the frozen communist hell, he died in the Gulag at the age of twenty-nine.

My grandparents were born in Russia—they emigrated during the Second World War. When I was fourteen, my parents took me to Russia for a visit that stretched for more than a month. I vividly remember many places but most of all Moscow and the Red (Beautiful) Square with the hulking Kremlin Towers in the background. Red Square is famous for many dramatic events of Russian history—demonstrations, riots, parades and executions.

I loved Russian culture all my life—in my youth, I even gave Marxism the benefit of the doubt. Walking the same streets as Pushkin or Dostoevsky? Awe-inducing.

My father wanted to swing by his place of birth—only a couple of miles off of our state-approved itinerary…he hadn't seen the place since they fled and had heard their main house was transformed into a school. Before we even drove a couple of miles off the itinerary they came after us with helicopters and police cars (monstrous Volgas) and told us to keep on the road and not to get off it again…I might have wet my pants…I'll never forget it. My father never did get to see his birthplace.

The story I heard from my grandmother is about her younger brother—who witnessed Stalin's burial and funeral service in Red Square, formerly known as the Cabbage Market before the Russian Revolution (called November 7 Square after). He and his friend courted serious trouble during the service because they were caught laughing.

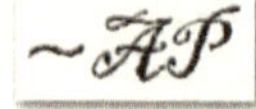

When Stalin Died, We Laughed

As they laid Joseph Stalin's coffin and lifeless body in the mausoleum in Red Square, a rally of grief was going on. The historic Cabbage Market held a somber sea of people.

Important men from various enterprises and institutions were present. From a stage, specially built for this momentous occasion, men spoke and wiped blurry, teary eyes. Their speeches, drowned in pathos, were delivered with bullhorns that echoed across the vast market for everyone to hear. Men with black bands of mourning on their arms escorted girls, old and young, bearing headscarves and flowers. The crowds packed the square. The subdued crowd expressed pain and hid any other feelings they might have harbored.

Markets in other cities—in countries forming the CCCP (or USSR), and all other grand collections of communist camps—were linked to the events in the vast Red Square. When the big man, the great general, military genius, world leader, show-trial judge, executioner and air-brusher of history was submitted to eternity in the mausoleum, an announcement was made…the whole breathless world would honor the great man with a moment of silence. In that *silent moment* came the screaming sound of sirens from factories and horns from locomotives at the train station.

My friend pulled out his handkerchief and covered his face. His shoulders began to shake. Anyone not knowing him might think he cried uncontrollably, but I knew him well and recognized that laugh…the most contagious in the world. I started laughing too—with guttural roars but without a handy handkerchief to hide behind. Our laughter lasted ten long seconds. We committed sacrilege—a thoroughly and completely impertinent act. In large part, the screaming sirens masked our crime.

After the service, we were approached by two sincere young men—and guided away from the dispersing crowd toward police headquarters. A serious charge was placed upon us. We were called *irresponsible*, *enemies of the people,* and *counter-revolutionaries*. The comrade in charge of the police center came in to talk to us. We were very afraid and fully aware of our dire situation.

We were asked to explain our inexcusable behavior in the square.

My friend answered quickly.

"The instant we started our silence the sirens blared. We laughed because it was impossible for anyone to be quiet."

The comrade-in-charge studied us for a long moment.

"We must let them go. Don't you see they are mentally retarded?"

After a dismissive wave of his hand, we were pushed down the hallway, through a heavy door and into the street.

Our laughter was over for the day.

My uncle lived in Tel Aviv when I visited him fifteen years ago. He told me his story of escape during the war and his love for fourteen-year-old C who he never forgot even though M now holds his heart and has lived with him for the past twenty years. My uncle and his friend D were eighteen in 1943—trying desperately to fool the Gestapo during tough times in Düsseldorf. They hid in the building where fourteen-year-old C's parents had an apartment. At that time, both men were infatuated with her.

After forty years, in 1983, my uncle reconnected with his friend D—they decided to take a trip down memory lane…to close open circles and wounds. This story is inspired by his experience.

He died two years ago and my heart would not permit me to record the story until now…

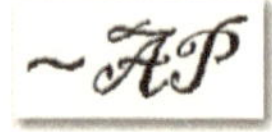

Nothing is Worth more than this Day

When D appeared at the hotel, he made me feel old. I was twenty years older than him. He had almost no white hair and few wrinkles. Most Israelis, stressed by permanent war and assaulted by the sun, age fast—I didn't expected to find him so fresh.

He came with his wife, a sweet German woman, which—I found out later—was more aware of our Hebrew traditions than he was. Our group of four went to see his father, who last saw me when I was a small child. We stopped in for just a few minutes—we were in a rush as D had reserved a table at an Italian restaurant. C waited for us—our plan was to pick her up on the way.

In the car I coughed something awful—I was nursing a cold. As we traveled, I coughed more and more—I could hardly articulate a word. M was quiet while D asked for details of the past; I answered between coughing fits, which increased in intensity. I did what I could to sound composed.

We were in a quiet residential area, with manicured trees and orderly parked cars…the stereotypical German fashion. D slid out of the car. We decided to stay behind. The tension was thick enough to cut with a knife; none of us moved. I wanted to run—to take a taxi back the hotel.

Excuses ran through my head. I wanted to be dismissed. I had a cold and I did not want everyone to get sick. I could barely breathe.

What was M thinking?

So many kilometers, so many thoughts, and my cough that won't stop…maybe I'm dreaming. Maybe I'm someone else. Maybe I'll wake up, but it dawned on me—I did not recognize the parking lot, it was probably built after I was last here…it couldn't be a dream.

D reappeared with a forced smile.

"C invited us for an appetizer."

The stairway was familiar. Lots of steps.

Over thirty years had passed and the stairs still rose, what do you know?

Obsessively, I counted the stairs while a poem from childhood drifted through my mind. At the doorway, I raised my eyes. Through a crack of door, standing on the threshold, she stood. Beautiful, unchanged.

We embraced and walked in the apartment. It was the same one her parents lived so many years ago. From the kitchen, C brought snacks and a bottle of white wine. I asked for a glass of water and an ashtray. Out on the terrace, I lit a cigarette, and looked at the trees—overcome with emotion, my hands shook.

I was alone, reliving my lost youth in Düsseldorf.

"You cough a lot—sounds awful. Smoke too much?" She stood beside me, her figure perfect with not one gram of extra weight. Her eyes bored into me as I tried to rest my eyes anywhere but on her. "I feel I must tell you something—an oath I swore in childhood. Is it okay to reawaken old memories? Messy memories that never die?"

I stayed silent.

We came in the living room and on a shelf—a photo of a little girl I knew. I was suspicious of her intention.

"Why did you put your old picture here?"

"It's my daughter—she looks a lot like me at that age."

I resumed my silence.

The restaurant was a cacophony of blabbering in German, English, and Hebrew. I sat in the front and coughed vigorously—trying not to talk. C found a common language with M, my girlfriend—a broken Hebrew and that made me laugh at the absurdity of life and our lost adolescence. So many years gone by and all of us so changed. In Düsseldorf, we lived such different lives than in Israel. We gossiped about friends from childhood—each in far corners of the world.

Who could imagine our destiny back in times when we were running and trying to cheat life?

In the car, traveling back to the hotel, I sat between C and M. We rode in silence, interrupted only by my annoying cough. Uncontrolled thoughts came to our minds.

Who is C today?

To stay ahead of the memories, I vowed to stay in Düsseldorf. We arrived at the hotel and disembarked, saying our good-byes and hugging. Her body pressed into mine and my mind went blank.

That night, I closed a circle.

* * * * *

The next day I made a big discovery—I can control unbidden thoughts.

* * * * *

We visited Düsseldorf and I loved every corner. Every street was a long dream—several times, I thought I saw C's slender shadow on the street.

M and I made up our minds to put aside tension and have a successful vacation. So it was. I led her on a tour of every area I remembered. The Harz Mountains, Goslar and Menden—where we were caught in a torrential rainstorm. Under a dripping awning, we talked to an old lady in German about Judaism and Christianity. I told her how life led me to Christianity—recognizing Jesus as Messiah, but she answered that Jesus does not require recognition. He is or isn't regardless of our opinion or dogma. We understood each other perfectly.

We drove through Gottingen, Kassel (where I had the luck to immerse myself in a Chagall exhibit), Wurzburg—then we changed the route. Leaving Nurnberg and Regensburg for another time, we focused on Munich.

Back home in Tel Aviv, I received a letter with a Düsseldorf return address. I opened it and C's name jumped into my eyes. Inside, a picture…a matronly woman over fifty with a little girl of fourteen standing next to her. A girl I knew, but had never met.

For a week, M and I avoided the subject. Foggy images overlapped broken lines. All of our shared moments were out of focus.

C and her circle were closed to me…now and forever.

The Magic Bird—A Fairy Tale

In a faraway country many years ago, lived a king with a young son.

Following the traditions of this land, when the prince reached maturity, he had to prove to the counsel of Wise Men surrounding the King that he had a nimble mind and was prepared to face the heavy affairs and challenges to the kingdom—like his father did for so many years.

For this challenge the young prince was required to solve a problem in an original and noteworthy way. The task was decided on in secrecy by the old men's council who hoped to observe the young prince's aptitude and judge how he would react to dangers to the kingdom.

What challenge did the counsel give the emperor's young son?

They asked him to draw a portrait of a nonexistent bird.

The prince asked for additional hints.

"If you ask me to draw a bird that does not exist then I could conclude such a creature could easily not be a bird at all."

"True," the wise men admitted. "Yet still, it is called a bird."

"Very well. If you ask me to do a portrait, that means that I should imagine and create an image..."

"True. But that does not change the task."

"For this portrait, I shall do as my heart dictates."

"We understand." The wise men approved. "That is exactly what we ask of you."

"I imagine a wonderful magic bird with feathers that grow like the beautiful petals of a flower. It could just as easily be called a flower."

"Yes, but it remains a bird," one of the wise men pointed out.

"This is how I would look at it: as flower *and* bird—it may not be judged by its sweet aroma."

The assembled crowd was restless.

"Do not stop. Continue, please," one of the wise men declared while striking his desk with a gavel.

"This flower of all flowers can live forever—when its petals start shedding, she transforms into a bird...literally, a miracle flower, but also a wonder-bird…a miracle that does not look like any other bird."

"This is hard to accept," exclaimed one of the older wise men.

"Silence. Let us see where he goes," intervened another.

"It is good you interrupt me so I can be reminded not to forget anything. The world's researchers all talk about this bird—known as the paradox-bird because her existence is mixed with her nest. The bird and nest are one and the same with the paradox-bird. As the ancients say, she is equally the road and traveler…the horse and horseman. She is the Gateway to the World, Mother of all seen and unseen—past, present and future. Humankind itself, as an ancient story goes, was hatched by the bird."

Among the Wise Men, the King coughed in his beard as a sign he approved of his son's bold explanation.

"To be well understood," the young prince continued, "nothing moves her but devotion. This bird is conquered only through love. She does not sing, but enjoys delighting all with her beauty."

A man representing the kingdom's ordinary citizens spoke.

"Tell us more."

"We should not scare the bird...we should approach her only with fondness. We should spoil her and entertain her with pure, warm-hearted love stories. In ancient history, the bird struggled with apocalyptic forces to free our greatness with the strength of her spirit. This is why it is a very patient creature, dreaming and seeing our future through her eyes, feeling our senses—laughing or crying when we are happy or sad."

"I don't understand how a bird can understand sadness," voiced a challenger.

"This bird is responsible for the history of humanity and therefore holds our sadness and joy in equal measures. Whether we are rich or poor, only this bird knows what we treasure forever."

"Well, there is no such bird," claimed a wise man, "so what use is this legend?"

"I was to paint a portrait of bird that does not exist. If the bird has a portrait, then it exists…unless you claim love and art and dreams are useless…"

In his time, the prince ascended to the throne and reigned over happy, prosperous people in his distant country.

Don't Mind the Naked Man on the Couch—Chapter Four

Love is a game…a fun game of catch-me-if-you-can. Once playing starts, you must take turns getting caught. It is a basic principle; if you want to be loved, you have to let yourself caught.

She never let Michael win so he never loved her. Larry thought he won but didn't, so he didn't matter.

She was a tough child who wore either long white socks or nothing.

Her emotions had the intensity of a raging fire. Air, with all due respect, vibrated with her beating heart. She was sure she'd go to hell but something made her think she could change before it was too late. In hell, your desires are never satisfied. That's what they say.

Was she scared?

Yes, maybe. She cut her life against the grain.

On a shelf in her living room, she kept a gray box filled with letters and old photos. Never sentimental—she fought hard against the emotion. But, every so often, she'd open the box. Its contents were like Seurat paintings with multitudes of seemingly-random dots coming together as faces, words, and memories. They stirred a unique feeling in her belly, like an itch that could not be scratched.

Her blue eyes matched pieces of the big puzzle—fitting faces to words and the reverse. She turned a postcard or photo in her hands and read the few lines on the back. Some she barely remembered, some she knew by heart.

"Friday evening. Friday. Wait for me."

The postcard had a mountain landscape on the front and his signature on the back.

Matilda was sixteen when she pushed her body in the dance of gestures—delicate and haphazard. The arc of her weird life formed a parabola. She came back to everything left behind. Sixteen and enslaved by Saul's textured complexity. Saul, a dark, Machiavellian man with glowing, controlling green eyes.

Twenty years prior, in a wooden cabin surrounded by woods and mountains, an innkeeper shouted something about a storm. Matilda did not care. She stared at the woods with intense persistence—trying to match the green mountains of the postcard's cover with the twilight view displayed in front of her as real life. When she held the postcard and quickly looked towards the sun setting behind the mountains it almost looked like the image was fixed in place. But an errant rock or incongruous slope, unmatched in the postcard, interfered.

A voice came from behind her.

“Close one eye, then switch to the other—you can get it.”

A heavy hand fell on her shoulders. Behind her was Saul—in murky shadows and looking rough as if after a long hike. He seemed preoccupied and rushed, but his gestures were soft and his voice velvety.

“Come on...come in, a storm is coming.”

Her nostrils caught the ionic smell of electricity. She wanted to stay and watch.

She responded with unwanted uncertainty in her voice.

“I like the rain and wind…I like the feel of danger.” Inside, with unnecessary loudness, the innkeeper closed the shutters. Increasingly insistent, the wind whined. Her voice was as quiet as a whisper. “It will be a wonderful storm.”

Thunder. Angry, untamed clouds broke above the cabin. The shutters strained at their hinges.

Thunder burst between them and attacked shelves bearing an army of lined-up bottles—they clanked like an absurd percussive concerto. The roof seemed to be attacked by drunken carpenters. With a second bout of thunder, the deafening storm rushed by fast and furious.

Afterward, she watched him sit at the base of a tree and smoke a cigarette. Beyond the trees, the moon and stars sprouted. It was late, terribly late. She sat next to him with her knees raised to her chin.

He smiled at her.

"What causes the stars to appear and disappear?"

She answered with a laugh.

"It's the job of a naughty girl to light them with a magic wand as repentance for past mistakes."

White socks loosely rode her thin ankles and emphasized the contours of her faultless legs. The image led to thought, thought to excitement, and excitement to the sin of unhindered desire. With an artist's skill, he kindled warmth in her belly.

Desire.

Intense emotions vibrated and flowed between them.

* * * * *

Life's tragic events clear the spirit. Later on, that's what she was told.

Her memories were like trains. Some screamed by quickly while others were heavy with travelers. Some were routed to forgotten siderails…fenced in and neglected. Driverless, with broken windows—rusty and desolate. She could not scrap them. They were vestiges of her life. We would be nothing without remembered people and events.

Some trains start a long journey but end up abandoned.

She reviewed images recorded long ago and felt things, perhaps imagined, as frightfully real hallucinations. She took comfort in false security—

that dead history was safely in the past and could not touch her.

During her mental wandering she grasped who she might be…flesh and bones, soul and spirit or perhaps just a random thought in God's feverish mind.

Her life was a gray box filled with old letters, postcards and photographs. In the storm's aftermath, Saul sat at the base of a tree and gazed with animal lust at the white socks embracing her tanned ankles.

What do *you* think causes the stars appear and disappear?

Gravity keeps us locked to the ground. However, in love's outer space, there is no gravity. Your heart floats free and drifts. That's what love meant to me as I happily floated through life feeling luckier each and every day.

I loved you because you were intelligent and well-spoken—you filled a gap in my life.

I remember you. No matter your name—you left footprints on my heart no amount of scrubbing can clean away…

We composed quiet symphonies around our names.

A black sack made me think back—when someone I once loved lived in a house full of my things. Sick of them, she wanted them gone and decided to dispose of them. She put them in a black bag and shipped them out—a victory over a painful past and a quest for imaginary freedom.

Memories permeate the fabric of our lives.

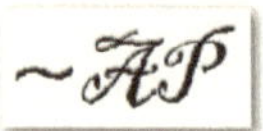

Queen of Dust

The car stopped in front of me. It was written in his eyes…the driver looked as if he knew me from childhood, but no longer knew my name.

You grew up. I don't know what to call you.

He said nothing while hauling the van's cargo door open. Using strong arms, he picked up a black bag—and dropped it at my feet. He climbed back in the driver seat and shifted gears. Soon, he was gone.

I looked at the bag, feeling puzzled.

How did he know I was the beneficiary of the package? How did he know where to find me? Who has a reason to send me such a thing?

It was black plastic bag, weighing about fifty pounds.

Too many questions. Not enough answers.

I lit a cigarette and sat on the edge of the sidewalk. The afternoon sun pureed air, asphalt and concrete. Suddenly, I remembered…we met in a bar that reeked of cheap beer and testosterone…around the corner from my rented room. Your face bore a confused expression when I offered to run off the guy irritating you with awful pickup lines. The man was clueless—cheap and offensive.

"I bought a bottle of wine," I said, "and asked for two glasses—hoping you'd prefer intelligent discussion to the cacophony emitted by the tactless man harassing you."

While awaiting your reply, I imagined how would it feel to ski on a steep slope—swishing and swooshing with dizzying speed…as quick as suicide.

"Wait. I'll go to the bathroom and then we'll talk," you said.

Between that response and the halfway mark of my cigarette—three years. Good times, though the years stretched like the complex dance of a contortionist ballerina from an imaginary circus. Surreal images from a movie we watched together.

We shared quiet moments…moments I loved. Other memories were less welcome because they signaled the prophetic alchemy of ill coming our way.

If I put my hands on the back of my head and close my eyes I can see myself back in time—when, three weeks after our first kiss, I moved in with arms full of boxes…moving from one prison to another. A well-intended transfer, though later on, my departure to Germany and the message I left triggered your extreme jealousy and pathological victim syndrome. Clues about what was to come...

What was to come really came. We loved each other loudly—with screaming and stomping—raising clouds of dust during crazy, beastly love-making sessions. I feasted on our devotion, peeling shedding layers from our souls; each emotion carefully exfoliated—shedding putrid stratum like a stale onion. We were poisoned by our shared anguish.

Once we tried to paint over the stink of cigarettes we smoked together. Washing away the smell of my sweat on your sheets and the folds of your bed would be equally impossible. My touch perforated your skin and let your human essence escape.

The black plastic bag on the sidewalk seemed to hold all my sins and transgressions. In the bar where we met, I drank a second glass of wine, then another and another. Later, two weeks in Switzerland raced by like grassfire. In Geneva, I was dizzy after spending £40 for a drink and a jar of pickled asparagus.

The details are too many to linger on…three years passed as dangerous traffic flowing before a stranded pedestrian. Dust settled on our past—a fine powder hiding everything. Or, maybe just on you…the Queen of Dust…born in the desert of my recollection.

As I finished my pack of cigarettes, my thoughts were silent songs. I thought of the black swan of despair spreading dying wings. No one is evicted benignly from the land of big love; there is always a vaguely-remembered man in a van dropping a black-plastic bag of history at your feet. You need a surgeon's detachment from your feelings or you'll drown in sad plasma...a transfusion from the two hearts that once beat as one.

"Wrong address, buddy," I mumbled after the van drove away. I crossed the street to Vis-à-Vis Bar where the bartender served a bitter cocktail I'd tasted too often.

In love, as in war, the winners are those who will not accept peace.

Ghost Words and other Echoes…

Do not weep; do not wax indignant. Understand.
- Baruch Spinoza

My emotions form an intricate labyrinth between heart and action. I struggled, year-after-year, to weave a life from an uncompromised state of being—to maintain a pure heart despite various detours terminating in emotional cul-de-sacs.

People speak charms and incantations—some eat right and work out, and others educate themselves or worship a higher being, but we create and re-create ourselves daily. I live and hurt by my own doing or undoing. Somehow I convinced myself in the midst of life, albeit reluctantly, that life comes and goes the way I made it to be. I ignorantly lived in tacit acceptance of what turned out to be the sordid and vulgar side of *for better or worse*.

After every fork, plate and piece of furniture was counted and divided…I discovered in the deafening silence of my newfound solitude an openness to hurt, insult and bitterness.

I wrote a couple of stories wrapped around infidelity…hoping for the pain to fade away.

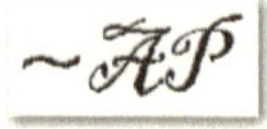

The Revenge

He is thirty-four years old and does not show signs of being a creepy character. He is overweight, but often thinks of himself, when walking down the street, as disgustingly fat. Fat and bald, the lack of hair around his temples highlights his big forehead. He looks like an accountant should. Name? Caesar. Like Gaius Julius Caesar—the Roman general and emperor.

Half a year prior he had the misfortune of discovering his wife was cheating on him. She did not know he knows because he decided not to immediately collect his revenge. He did not insult her with names like *bitch*, *slut*, or *whore*…he continued accounting, adding penny after penny. He honored obligations to the treasury, and thus to the country, while she, his wife, came home late in the evening giggling—full of post-coital glee.

Three months after witnessing his cheating wife with her lover, he emerged from shock and decided to pursue his revenge…to lure her and her lover in the basement, lock the door behind them and then conveniently lose the key. No one would know they were there—buried alive in the back yard of the villa only five hundred yards from the house but far away from the neighbors. He thought about this plan and every time, a freakish smile blossomed on his overstuffed, sweaty face.

He needed a reason to get her in the basement so he built a bar. The cellar was unused before; he went to work installing a counter under thick-glass shelves and mirror surrounded by a string of Christmas lights discovered in the attic. In front of the counter he arranged two spindled stools. So the cellar bar would look real, he lined up bottles—elegant, expensive, and irresistible. Caesar knew she would come down with her lover.

Caesar sits—his massive body perched on one of the stools. He holds his tiny glass between chubby fingers and thinks of many more things to put in place for the plan. He swirls cognac around his mouth and shivers with pleasure while idly counting the Christmas lights. Bored, he moves on to counting the bottles.

Eight bottles on three shelves.

Plus eight in the mirror, sixteen. Bottles of different configurations, sizes, and colors. Suddenly he frowns.

Eight?

With the one on the counter—nine.

Where is the tenth bottle? Did he drink it?

No…he allowed himself only one bottle for a glass every Saturday when he stops by. Counting every indulgent sip is part of an accountant's way of life. The last constellation he arranged was: one bottle on the bar, three bottles on the top shelf, three on the middle shelf, and three on the bottom shelf—all spaced evenly.

Now the bottom shelf holds only two bottles—missing the one in the middle. He thinks of all sorts of nonsensical explanations: thieving ghosts, leprechauns, and a thirsty octopus.

He feels very alone in the cellar. It's too quiet…too much cold comes from hidden gaps in the foundation. The silence emanating from under the counter is too deep. The gap between the two bottles on the bottom shelf seems huge. After several minutes of discomfort, he decided to leave.

His body felt massive and solid while climbing the stairs. Pushing the heavy metal door, he breathed more heavily from panic than exertion. The door remained immobile…beads of cold sweat sprouted on his brow. He pushed harder, but the door was sealed shut—like the entrance to a crypt.

Peeking through the bars covering the tiny window next to the door, he saw his wife and lover walking away…toward the cottage. She wore jeans, a knee-length coat, a black hat on her head and a yellow handkerchief wrapped around her neck. Her lover seemed agitated…vibrating in his thin jacket. He carried the missing bottle. They approached the back door—where her lover politely held the door open for her. They disappeared inside without looking back.

Caesar descended to the bottom of the stairs and looked around the cellar.

Now, he would need a new plan for revenge.

Three-Minute Sex

It was a very hot summer day. Even when night arrived, everything still smoldered. On the sidewalks, people drowned in sweat.

Except for her—sprawled across the bed waiting for him. She waited more than an hour in a studied pose—dipped in spicy perfume and perspiring from the heat—playing music said to have magnetic, erotic powers.

Missing? A man to attract. Erotically.

The corpses of six cigarettes in the ashtray and no knock at the door. No knock. Not even an accident of wind or a child playing in the hall.

She wanted to change her mind and leave but something in her remained hopeful.

He called the next day and apologized—he had many excuses.

What was the point?

On the phone, his words were a mumble. Not because the connection was bad but because she didn't care.

"I was...I arrived…they had…"

"No," she said before hanging up.

Breaking up can be liberating. People tend to hold a relationship like treasure.

Why bother?

It's more pleasant to be alone.

Why worry about what was said yesterday?

If yesterday you said *love*, then today you have to continue saying *love*. But to have loved yesterday and today no longer feel love—to falsely smile or make sarcastic sweet talk—communicating instead as if there were no kind words left in the world…that is not love. Breaking up is human nature. People, women in particular, spend their time creating love, but too many of them share it with someone who does not show up. He doesn't show up because he knows he'll be forgiven.

But she did not want to be a fountain of forgiveness. She wanted sex. She wanted sex yesterday and he didn't show up...

She looked at the golden sky.

It's too hot for sex, other than, maybe…the quick, three-minute type of sex.

But that's not something she could ask. It would require a man she knew well—a man she was comfortable with.

"Listen, I want sex. But only three minutes, no more."

A man you barely knew would look at you funny and would take you for, for…who knows? There was no one she could think to ask. In frustration, she picked up a newspaper and saw that a famous tiger had returned to the city zoo.

I'll go see the tiger.

The zoo was packed with too many mothers herding misbehaving children.

Children are not allowed to stick fingers in their nose in public.

But, here in this foreign land, none of the mothers knew or cared.

She looked for a sign to see if she was allowed to smoke. No sign. She took this as permission and lit a cigarette in front of the tiger. Young, but he had the dead eyes of a zoo tiger. She knew the eyes of a wild animal—they looked nothing like this tiger's eyes.

He looked directly at her and had the good sense to be ashamed of his captivity. She looked back, but not as an admiring a fan like the surrounding idiots.

You couldn't even fight the move from one cage to another.

The tiger, close to the bars, slid his nose through. Mothers and children drew back in fear.

The tiger looked up at her in submission.

Well, not really. Of course not.

From behind bars the story changes. She blew smoke in the tiger's face—he did not flinch. He looked at her as if the smoke was punishment he had to bear for not fighting.

The next day it rained—she was happy. With the tiger in her mind…free, with rain all around.

She thought about going back to the zoo, but she didn't have enough money so she didn't.

Instead, she went to *him* and knocked at the door.

He was in his underwear. Taut body, handsome.

"Listen carefully," she said. "Want to have sex? For three minutes?"

"Three minutes?"

"Yes, that's what I want. Okay?"

"Okay."

She entered the bedroom, got naked, and waited for him to get naked too. He grabbed her hair and whispered something unintelligible—nothing that interested her.

It took over two minutes.

Silently, while he watched in drowsy despair, she got dressed and left. Outside, the rain cooled her sweat and cleansed her thoughts.

She never got everything she wanted—sometimes, she didn't get *anything* she wanted. She didn't want to be the tiger. But, maybe she was...

The Pain Killer

After being kicked out of heaven, Adam made a discovery. The best way to cope with the pain that accompanied being cast out of the garden was to take a pill. But, he was unsure what kind of drug his ache required.

Film-coated tablets, encapsulated, or something injected?

Confused, Adam plowed the ground and procreated while Eve delivered babies without anesthesia. Oral analgesics were invented many centuries later—after Eve was finished with her fertile cycles. A flood swept through and a new civilization bloomed.

Today, Adam is Larry, or Billy, or Joe and lives close by in a suburb in your century and your year. Unfortunately, he has a headache. Fortunately, the painkiller was invented. The new Adam sits up in bed with pain banging around in his head. He mumbles and pulls himself from his cradle and sorts through a drawer where medicine and prescriptions fill tubes—white powders, medicinal liquids and pills.

His purpose was bamboozled when his eyes brushed over the Catholic calendar on the wall. With his hands in the drawer, he began thinking.

According to Catholic dogma, are painkiller pills forbidden in the days of Lent?

Pills are not meat, cheese, milk, or eggs, so why should they be prohibited?

Man is allowed to be pain-free throughout Passion Week, right?

It's a tacit agreement between God and man—tasks and duties for both parties. God has to watch over man (which he does) and man has to multiply and fill the earth (which he does, albeit haphazardly).

Our modern Adam cannot procreate. The skull-splitting headache precluded breeding-oriented activities. This situation started two months earlier.

He looked at his wife lying asleep in bed…she was surely consumed by dreams of procreation. Standing and staring with envy at the bed he abandoned for a pill—with a sweaty hand groping the knob, he fumbled through boxes and bottles until he found the headache cure. For a while, at the beginning of his trip of pain, he thought about jumping from the balcony as a means relief but concluded a pill would work fast enough. The last time he took a pill, he got a stomachache on top of the pain in his head. He should protect his stomach before taking a pill.

Fresh dilemma. Headache or stomachache?

The drawer was a step sideways from his wife's purse; his pain permitted him to violate her privacy. With two fingers he quietly opened the bag. Among many objects inside—nail polish, two tubes of lipstick, a tiny screwdriver, half a sandwich, an invitation to the theater, two hair clips, a glue stick, keys to the cellar—was a phone number written with blue ink on the back of a twenty-percent-off coupon for a cyber cafe.

His head was ready to explode. Looking at his wife sleeping…then at the things in her purse. For a few moments, his eyes scooted from the purse back to her. The phone number mocked him.

In the last few days, he noticed a chill in her mood; a practiced nonchalance.

Despite the late hour, he grabbed the phone, punched in the numbers written on the back of the coupon and waited a couple of seconds only to hear a voice on the other end. A male.

"Who's this?" Adam asked.

"I'm a pharmacist!" the male voice answered.

Maybe his wife was sick but did not want to burden him with more worries.

"Can, you recommend a gastric buffer for a pain pill?"

"Do you know what time it is?"

The man's voice held a grumpy tone.

"Yes, but I've been in pain for hours. Can you recommend a natural gastric buffer? I am the husband...of my wife. I think you know her."

"Try drinking milk," the man said before disconnecting.

The busy signal hummed with the painful throb in his temples. He put the paper with the phone number back in her purse.

Maybe she'll need medical advice.

Currently nothing hurt her, to his knowledge. He heard a guttural voice. She was awake and noticed her purse was moved two inches from where she left it.

"Have you been in my purse? Why did you mess around in my purse?"

"My head hurt and I wanted something to protect my stomach before I took a pain killer."

"And what did you find? I have nothing for your stomach."

"Milk is a good buffer. Thank God for the pharmacist."

He stood next to the refrigerator holding the carton of milk and could not help but notice a trickle of water on the floor. For head pain, it's good to know milk is a buffer when taking painkillers.

But the thread of water from under the refrigerator? Why didn't she have the telephone number for a plumber in her purse?

That way she could demonstrate she cared about the house, her family and important domestic problems like the leaking of a faulty refrigerator. With a plumber's phone number in her purse, she could show she cared for their house.

She could show she cared for him.

Life is uncomplicated, lacking complexities more often than not but when it comes to my take on it, I have a knack for tailoring Byzantine crafted plots around every moment I experience. Maybe it is inherited—in my genetic makeup from my colorful and never-boring family.

In Syria, when I was fourteen, my mother and I witnessed a hotel explode at the hands of an angry, vengeful faction. It didn't have much impact on me back then, but later in life, as I searched for an identity anchor in a sea of obscurity, the event popped into my memory as a story that practically wrote itself.

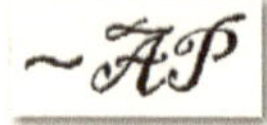

The Wedding Ring

Tired, he signaled the waiter for the bill. After glancing at his watch, he was surprised to see it was three A.M.

The room's thick cigarette smoke bothered his eyes; oriental music throbbing in the background was annoying and disturbed his craving for silence. The music repeated a sorrowful refrain with a languid rhythm. He threw a bored look around. The atmosphere, still lively for this late hour, was bizarre because of the patrons…a peculiar assembly of characters haunted this tiny bar on the border between two worlds. He felt as if he looked through a kaleidoscope at an inhuman landscape.

Young men in groups spoke stridently, most likely about football—he could not make out the Arab dialect...soldiers spending their mercenary money on drinks...prostitutes wearing garish makeup and scanty attire being closely watched from a discreet distance by attentive pimps...whores and customers—couples for the night or the week, seeking artificial intimacy...men like him, men alone, drowning loneliness in alcohol; solitary and absent from things happening around them.

Irritated, he looked toward the waiter, but could not catch his eye. The next sound he heard was the vivid, live clink of crystal glasses. A quick look back…for a second, time dilated.

A harsh, noisy, careless world desperate for understanding.

Gestures missing, noise but no sound.

Only eyes, which, until then, he'd paid no attention to—now filled with mad excitement and intensely seeking answers to their distress. The world was a sea of opaque eyes, as if imaginary atropine dilated and paralyzed them—allowing fear to spread throughout the room.

Visceral howling brought the world and time back to present. In a fractured second, the room exploded in pieces of furniture, cutlery, pots, food, and personal belongings. He jumped with the others, but the movement was frozen; he remained standing. It was only a second's hesitation but enough for torrents of bodies to frantically rush the only possible escape.

A woman's face appeared in a twitch of lucid consciousness—mad foresight—and he understood what to do…not to act on instinct and run. Instead, with a quick gesture, he took off Corinne's ring a couple of seconds before the room pulverized.

Then he spotted her. As something you catch with your eye in the space appearing intermittently between cars of a fast train…she stood, frozen like him. Young, so young...in the bustle, their eyes met and fugitive questions were answered.

She smiled.

A second of silence, then all cells screamed; his brain exploded into a million synapses of pain. It became dark...

When he woke, it was still dark. He had a weird sense of feeling nothing—no up, no down, no pain. Only pressure without anything discrete on his body. He was caught in a formless trap. He could move one hand. Though unhindered, the rest of the body remained inaccessible.

I'm done for...

He felt no remorse…no fear.

He explored the encircling dark. It was as if his body didn't exist—never existed. He moved his fingers but felt nothing, just dust...so much dust.

Soon his hand responded better to commands...his fingers became more aware of things on the floor. He felt a soft blanket of dust, gravel and then, unexpectedly, the small metal circle.

Corinne's ring...

His soul bled with the first regret. Disparate images moved before his eyes. He wanted to be buried next to her in the shady cemetery with limestone markers, massive, shadowy chestnut tree, iron benches put there by who knows. He remembered her voice and her timid approach to making love.

But now he was in a foreign country under a mountain of rubble—what was once a mediocre restaurant on the border. Unknown, unknown...it grew dark again.

He woke to a wail. A low moan...he explored with his fingers, his only contact with the surrounding reality. Dust, and more dust, he was immersed in an endless sea of dust.

Then he found a hand. A warm hand. He felt the fingers, palm, and sought a pulse. He felt it. Weak, intermittent...almost extinguished, but there. His soul filled with joy riding on sadness. She was also a prisoner in the rubble—adrift in the space between life and death. Her fingers—her thin wrist did not move.

"Can you hear me? Hello?"

His mouth was full of debris and blood—a new spurt of blood came with each attempt to move his tongue.

"Miss...can you hear me?"

A weak moan—then the hand he held came alive. He squeezed and received an immediate response. Their hands remained clasped...the only link between two held captive by the darkness.

"How are you, Miss? How do you feel?"

"Never better."

He could not resist a smile. Her humor sent a ray of sunshine into his soul. With fondness and gratitude, he squeezed her hand.

"Are you in pain?"

"I do not feel anything except for your warm hand...I think I am very damaged..."

He heard her laugh or imagined it.

"What's your name, Miss?"

"Alana...I think my name is Alana..."

“I am Matthew. Uh, I mean, my name is Matthew...”

“What happened to us?”

“Don’t worry, Alana, they will come...they’ll find us…”

His voice sounded false, lacking confidence and certainty—hopeless.

“No, I do not think so. Matthew...”

Hands held each other.

“Why didn’t you run, Alana? You had time...”

He reviewed recent images. Sitting at the bar, they were immune to the chaos around them, unconcerned about the crowd and panic.

“How can you run from your life?”

He smiled—he liked her nonsequitur.

“You are so young…so…” he stopped.

He wanted to say beautiful…

“You’re nice,” she whispered. She continued without intonation. “I’m a rent-wife, a prostitute, Matthew.”

Did his hand leap? Oh, how he wanted not to startle her.

However, he was unsure…his fingers curled around hers and closed. With fingers on her thin wrist he felt her weakening pulse.

“Alana...Alana!”

No answer…

“Alana, Alana, stay with me, stay with me...please.”

The only sounds from his blood-filled, debris-choked mouth were whispers and wheezing. Her hand remained still; he heard her voice as though through dream.

"I'm tired, Matthew."

"Don't fall asleep…"

His hand squeezed hers but she'd passed out. Her pulse fluttered, chaotic, while she sank in lethargy—a dreamless sleep.

Both of them woke at faint noises coming from somewhere or nowhere above them.

"You hear, Alana? We are saved."

This time his voice sounded encouraging—happy and filled with hope.

"Matthew...yes, I hear…"

Her voice was sad—drowned in despair. To his surprise, he realized their hands no longer communicated. Devoid of emotion and joylessly waiting.

The voices were closer…but they sounded different.

Reality painted itself clearer…neither wanted to be saved, they both wanted to die. His brain revolted at the thought while his soul embraced peace. Years prior, he prayed for his bitter end—he fought with God and asked this world to forget about him…but her?

So young, so...should he say it again? Beautiful. She was so young and beautiful…why didn't she want life, light, heat, emotion?

She *had* to live. He wanted her to live. He needed to do something so she could live...

More noises, powerful and increasingly close, intruded on his thoughts.

"Matthew, it's inevitable…"

She cupped his fingers with a reassuring gesture.

They would save a dog before they'd save a whore. And then, glimpsing the preordained, he remembered…the wedding ring. A symbol of life and death—a wholesome icon of humanity. His hand searched through the carpet of dust. He found the metal circle.

He found her finger; the band slid on easily…it fit perfectly.

"You are a good man, Matthew. You are the best man I ever met…"

He had nothing to say. Nothing. From above, the noise nearly deafened them. Sounds could be identified and differentiated. The first was a sledgehammer...then the noise of pickaxes…he heard dogs barking. Then voices again. Increasingly close—the noises became words. Some he did not understand...but others, though shrouded in dissonance, were clear.

"…American team…hello…anybody…"

He wanted to shout, to say that she was there, that she expected them, that she was close, and that she should be saved. She must live… His mouth was full of debris, dust, and blood. He couldn't speak. Everything was silent.

A male voice.

"Here…right over here...come, come…it's a woman…"

Many talked at once. Someone repeated a question, irritating, but she could not distinguish it…then a voice with clear enunciation.

"No, no…this one's married…she's wearing a wedding ring…come on people…move, move, she's still alive."

The activity increased.

"Let go of his hand…let go…do you understand? Let go of his hand…he's dead, ma'am, I'm very sorry…let go now."

A bright light streamed through.

"Hey, I hear…hey. Lady…can you hear me? How are you doing? How are you?"

"Never better."

"You're in pain, ma'am?"

"No, I don't feel any pain. I don't feel anything."

"What's your name?"

"Alana, my name is Alana…"

"Let go of the hand…let him go…you know? Let go of the hand…lady, he—your husband is dead. I'm very sorry…you have to let him go."

Ghost Words and other Echoes…

When I turned fourteen, my mother took me on a trip meant to signify my coming-of-age; to increase my spiritual awareness and connection with my ancestors. We traveled to the Promised Land and spent three months roaming the vestiges of our civilization—we traveled through the desert, meditated on Mount Sinai and often listened to uncles and aunts recounting the story of my family's flight from the implosion of post-war Europe.

Story after story fed my imagination.

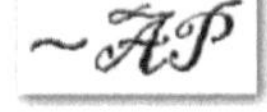

Desert Dream

Everything you can imagine is real.
- Pablo Picasso

Camels walked; sand wafted along the line. The sunset painted a sea of flames on the horizon. Everyone's gaze rested on the sun's dissolving disk.

The guide gave the signal and camels stopped. They kneeled for the millionth-time to let their passengers—their unwelcome burden—easily reach the hot sand.

Soon after, the bright disc disappeared behind the dunes—greedily swallowed by the ravenous desert—leaving the horizon steaming in the distance. The travelers looked for Scheherazade, discreetly at first, then more openly. When it was clear she was not with them, disappointment lived in their eyes.

Probably moved to a different caravan with other travelers. Perhaps a happier one, or maybe she searched somewhere else.

After looking for her every night, they knew her familiar habit. She attended to all who crossed the desert.

Scheherazade was missing from the convoy...

The blue-eyed man talked first. "How much more, chief? Is there…"

The chief cut him short.

"That is not the question I expected."

He looked straight ahead; piercing the settling gloom in search of unknown paths the caravan could follow the next day.

"We've been going for so many days, months, years—who knows anymore—and you haven't learned to ask the right question." The chief spoke with a quiet voice—as if trying not to disturb the peaceful sweetness of the freshly-fallen night.

The blue-eyed man looked at the tips of his shoes, and then at his wind-chafed, sun-scorched hands. He felt a lump in his throat—resentment.

What a stupid question to ask, the chief thought. Why couldn't he be quiet?

But the blue-eyed man did not remember asking the question any another time.

It was unfair for the chief to put him on the spot. And, who named him chief?

He could not remember.

The others swallowed their questions.

Better to remain silent.

Besides, Scheherazade was not here.

The blue-eyed man tossed his blemished pride aside. “Does the oasis really exist?”

“Yes,” the chief said, “and you may drink clear water from its well…not all of you, but some.”

His voice seemed to come from the deep.

Only some of us...why didn’t he say that before we all got so deep in the desert?

His hands nervously sweated into the stock of his shotgun.

Who is this guy to mock our lives? Who granted him answers to all the secrets of world?

The blue-eyed man’s thoughts spun rapidly in his tired mind.

“Effendi[1], let go of the shotgun. There’s no use for it here…no flying birds or dangerous animals hiding in the night. We’re the only ones here…though always fewer.”

A mutter traveled around the ring of tired people huddled around the fire.

Fewer? What does he mean by that? All of us are here, not any less or any more. This chief is strange.

He shivered as if a frozen hand stroked his back—his body shook from head to toe as he gazed into the fire.

Scared.

The fire cast creepy, dancing shadows into the pitch-dark night. The barrel of the shotgun gleamed.

“Did you drink that water?” the blue-eyed man asked.

---

[1] ‘Effendi’ means lord or master and is a title of respect—roughly equivalent to ‘sir’.

"I'm not here to drink the water," the chief said without turning around. "I'm just a guide…"

The blue-eyed man wished Scheherazade was with them.

"Chief, if you think we're safe, I need sleep," he said while arranging the shotgun at his side.

"Peace to you, Effendi, and beautiful dreams," replied the chief, moving for the first time since climbing off the camel. His hand touched his mouth and then his forehead as he released a greeting to his God. He stared into the darkness.

What hurts me, Effendi, is that tomorrow you will know the answer to your question and you'll brandish your shotgun and ask how much farther we'll travel while I know we'll never reach any destination. With each day—there are fewer and fewer us.

When will you know there is no oasis, Effendi? When will you understand? In the desert of your soul you are alone. I do not lead you to the oasis...you drive me. When will you understand, Effendi?

The blue-eyed man fell asleep in a desert without dreams, birds, or eyes shining in the night.

Sleeping with the oasis in his mind, a place he stubbornly believed in…and sought from the very beginning of his conscious life. He heard the beloved story while still a child. The oasis holds the purest water in the world, the deepest and cleanest…one drop could save you; one sip brings everlasting happiness. Many enthralled people believed Scheherazade's story. It was also said…in this oasis the love of a beautiful girl is born...a girl from the sea.

A sea, an oasis, a girl, a continent of love...nice story...but what of the girl's love?

The tale ended at this point. Maybe her love disappeared into the darkness of time.

He always felt he should seek this oasis as his only goal, as his only wish…but what if he never reached it? What if the chief is right and they will be fewer and fewer until the end? What if he is not among the final, chosen few?

For the blue-eyed man, the oasis road was endless. Another night passed with the senseless, echoing question raised in his thoughts while his hands cradled the shotgun.

The night passed quickly—the day brought the same thoughts and questions. The desert wind transported to his ears a girl's whisper, a crystalline singing of lost love. Sad, but joyous all at once—a slow song with beautiful lyrics.

The blue-eyed man knew the oasis existed; the eternal sea-girl lured all thirsty travelers like him.

He gained a new faith. For the first time since the beginning of the journey, he smiled…believing the oasis was there…there. The story's dream girl, the sea, and the song. He just wished he could talk to Scheherazade and share his vision.

The morning was like all the others. Desert, shrinking and expanding shadows of camels under the scorching sun and the slow, steady pace of the caravan commanded by the chief. Their clear, simple, unchanging, good leader. Faces chaffed by the wind, the sound of water sloshing in barrels.

The blue-eyed man counted his comrades. One, two…

The chief is right, there are fewer travelers…less than yesterday and less than the day before. How did he miss this?

Strange…

While gazing at the chief, the blue-eyed man's heart stopped. Like lightning, a guillotine sliced his perceptions. Another question came to his mind.

How long? Oh Lord, how long?

His heart restarted—flopping in his chest. His pulse hammered his ears with a crazy, dizzy rhythm. He closed his eyes and again, the question, like a razor-thin blade, sliced through his soul.

How long?

He took a deep breath, but air refused to fill his lungs. He opened his mouth to capture hot, invisible air but there was none. He pulled off his silk bandana and vest and unraveled his turban. Standing between camels, he sought the normal mechanics of life. Nothing. Choking in panic, dying of his own fear, swallowed by his phantom—he could do nothing.

I will die.

With that thought, calm overtook him. His heart stopped its murderous racing; he was filled with a sense of well-being. His empty lungs disavowed their needs. Images raced through his mind—memories—fresh and stale. His dry, cracked lips sprouted a smile. His heart pounded like a steam train. Air entered his lungs. He fell and felt sand against his body like a sea of flames. He took in greedy breaths, one after another.

He was alive. Still alive.

His camel, free, ran toward the front of the caravan. With a robust shout, the chief stopped the beast. He grabbed the leash and returned the animal to the blue-eyed man—who was sprawled in sand that tried to swallow him. The camel compliantly kneeled next to the fallen man. Possessed by a bizarre, unworldly feeling, he climbed back on the camel.

At the chief's command, the caravan was in motion again. The blue-eyed man was happy. He contemplated the arid surroundings with greedy eyes as if seeing the desert for the first time. His ears heard waves breaking on a shoreline. He smiled and closed his eyes. Behind his eyelids, the sea-girl smiled at him. Step-by-step, on wet sand, he followed her immortal footprints. The breeze brought to his nostrils the sweet smell of her wet hair. Her silhouette was lost in the distance while the sea swallowed her—as the desert swallowed her earlier. He opened his eyes.

I am not looking for an oasis—I'm looking for the sea.

The desert was alive—sparkling like a gigantic wave. It was a peculiar feeling, but beautiful. Trepidation overcame him. The oasis was a long stretch of beach filled with the essence of life and sand. On this shore lived a girl, whose story—only he knew.

A miracle, a mirage.

She was close. They stood, hand-in-hand, looking at the sea.

"Don't make a mistake, Traveler. Get on your camel and leave without asking questions."

"Why?"

In her sad eyes, he saw an eternal void where all light was absorbed…like a vortex…like a dark mirror.

Like one of Scheherazade's stories…

"You have a choice," the girl whispered, "you can still decide…"

In her eyes, he spotted two gems…two sparkles of light reflecting above her cheeks. Her mouth…red lips hid white, restless teeth. Her breath was scented. Fascinated, he grabbed her waist but the girl disappeared.

Magic.

Wet clothes and the taste of salt on his tongue.

The blue-eyed man opened his eyes. The sun baked the land…the obedient camel patiently kneeled. He raised the silk kerchief to his eyes to block the probing, relentless light.

And emerged from dream.

Don't Mind the Naked Man on the Couch—Chapter Five

Matilda had many questions and found so very few answers…she found no useful guidance in philosophy, sociology, psychology, science or religion—in fact, her studies added maddening complexity to her thoughts—the more she knew, the farther away ultimate answers seemed.

Her thoughts and recollections were incessant cries in a parallel universe; her thoughts were filled with crazy tangents.

How sweet the apple of truth?

How bitter the memories?

Why?

Living with the ins and outs of her mind, she discovered lost secrets in a gray box of letters and photographs.

Remember that November?

They sat in a car…Matt's arm was around her shoulders. His skin smelled faintly of guilt—basal, exciting guilt…voluptuous and indescribable.

The engine died and clicked while cooling. Possibilities filled the air.

She followed his eyes as they wandered up and down her legs.

"I'd like to know your story," he said.

Her voice was a whisper—as if her existence should be a secret.

"My story? What makes you think I have one?"

Later, they drank wine…slowly. With each sip, the tart liquid fueled their pleasure. Unhindered, lazy energies moved through bare, random patches of skin. The evening ended with cooling dampness and whispered conversation in the dark.

Her heart swelled with fiery cells. Passion crammed her mad pit of memories and hope filled her horizon like a fleeting glimpse of Mount Everest.

Why is passion always the cruel deceiver?

Whatever they had was faint, like drifting smoke from a faraway grass fire.

In bed, his eyes were closed against the morning light. The silent room felt deserted and filled with guilty stillness.

Matt's sensual eagerness could not completely banish Saul's ghost. After sex, Saul told her stories. Usually he claimed to be the living embodiment of the biblical Saul, but that did not stop him from making other equally unlikely claims, like being the literal offspring of Saul Katzenellenbogen, the mystical Polish temporary king…*rex pro tempore*. There was nothing temporary about Saul's imprint on her life, it was always present…like a watermark on expensive stationary.

She left Matt and walked ghostly streets guarded by tall trees with thick crowns…alley after alley after alley…thinking of nothing and everything.

In a dark doorway, a man pressed against a woman and a bottle clinked against the brick wall. His laughter sounded like Saul's, but it wasn't.

And, in a sky crowded with stars, she saw constellations like traces of footsteps—footsteps that disappeared when she blinked.

Humans have the tendency to sort and put things in order—to enumerate, alphabetize and create hierarchies in everything by dissecting, classifying, measuring and rating.

Everything gets measured—earthquakes and temperatures, mountains and rivers, raindrops and pop songs…oddly enough, there's even a hierarchy for angels. Everywhere you look, you'll find our omnipresent desire to force the world into structured echelons, like the misfit traveler mutilated to fit the mythical Procrustean bed. We are relentless in our avidity to count the world and put all things in their place.

In the legend of the Procrustean bed, an ancient giant lures weary travelers to his inn. While sleeping in his copper bed, he makes them fit. If they are too tall, he chops off their heads and feet—if they are too short, he painfully stretches their bones.

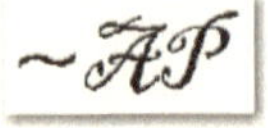

The Procrustean Bed—Part One

He walked on a dirty street.

After entering a doorway, he walked up rusty stairs in a miserable building before finding himself at her apartment.

The evening's darkness swallowed the town—light streamed through her curtains and cast ghostly shadows on the wall. He thought about everything followed by episodes of thinking about nothing…while sitting and staring at a random spot on the wall.

She waited on a bed that was too big for the room. No other furniture would fit in the small space where she lived her sordid life. A quick look at her reclining form on the mighty bed told him she was a slut, a whore...her life was punctuated by one heavy-breathing client after another.

Man after man, young and old, rich and poor, sweated and groaned in their release—oblivious to her implicit loneliness.

How could a whore have such a pretty figure?

How could a whore have such a lovely voice?

How could a whore whisper such sweet words?

How could a whore listen to him so intently?

How could a whore make him feel alive, and above all, how could a whore receive him in her bed and not ask for anything except money in return?

Tonight felt different from other nights—there was a light, sweet scent in the air. The fragrance of purity and grace.

She looked at him with big, black eyes. He was surrounded by the deep night of her pupils. He was in her darkness, but oddly, the space around him glowed with light when her frail arms touched his shoulders. Shaking, he put his hand on her cheek, and pressed against her.

He whispered. "…thank you…"

He felt the blow. Then another.

Blurry-eyed and bleeding, he understood. For the first time, she offered her home. He understood why she agreed to spend the night with him. He embodied the purity she slaughtered at night in dark alleys. He joined every villain passing through her life and understood in the end that no one would ever fit between the heavy wooden headboard and footboard of her procrustean bed.

On his final night, he felt a secret solidarity with many others who did not fit her bed—those who triggered her deep disappointment. That's why she'd been so kind to him. She knew he was on his last stretch, holding back the last howl of rage from her demon.

The bitch grew wings. He fought a smile while breathing in his last tremor of guilt. Shadows played on the wall as he quivered on the floor beside her bed. She slept quietly and peacefully.

Hanging on the wall—illuminated by flickering light—was an old painting in a wormwood frame.

An ageless portrait of a sly woman with deep, black eyes.

Adina Pelle

The Procrustean Bed—Part Two

"I am rich. I have become wealthy. I don't need anything." Yet you do not realize that you are miserable, pitiful, poor, blind, and naked.
Revelation, II I - 17

Walter stumbled into a different world—an unknown, insane Dionysian world of ritual madness and ecstasy. Men floated through the bar room like liquid ghosts…clustered in the center of the room, apparently at random, but in truth, bonded in constellations established before Walter showed up. Dancers writhed with intoxicated energy.

Visceral images…bodies in maddening contortions—bent over and wriggling…with musical slithering around a pole under the hungry looks of the depraved.

The music attacked Walter's ears—and became more vigorous and wild. He watched—in equal parts annoyed and mesmerized.

As the terminal heir of his noble family, it was given that he should behave in a suitable manner. A dignified manner.

Only an isolated, disturbed and sad life could explain his behavior.

Men, like a mindless herd, moved with anticipation toward the stage—closer to the gyrating, stimulating bodies. The dancers writhed as if possessed by lurid, irresistible forces.

That's when Walter noticed her dancing among kindred spirits—with red cheeks and quickened breath. Her thick black hair fell to her shoulders like rivers of night. She was as skinny and limber as a willow sapling. When her dark stare locked on Walter, he became the refreshing sip that satisfied her thirst.

He needed to escape the walls surrounding his truth…the facts of his righteous upbringing. His memories were filled with flitting images; pictures filled with pious sadness—cold, austere mental photographs. Madeline's sweaty dance released him. She was the master of the unspoken language of love. She wedged herself into his needy life. After each show, sensuously enveloping his dry, pallid body in the dark alleys around the bar.

After every release, late in the night after he closed his eyes, the fragrance of her warm body drifted through his senses. It was as if the country was bathed in smoke; her decadence was like a fruit, sweet and tender—scented by tamarind filling his nostrils…mingling with the gusty cheers of the men for whom she performed every night.

The ghosts in her eyes should have warned him of what was to come. She bedded him with feral rage…indulging her beastly appetites. Equally, he feared and cherished her implacable, cruel animal spirit while she feasted on the chambers of his soul.

The more he desired her warm, pliable body under him, the more she haunted him. Her voice echoed through the disintegrated and decomposed hollows of his spirit. She bled his senses dry.

His family never talked about the indiscretions of the common man. Madeleine made him feel important and desired. He was permitted to lose his identity—the heavy anchor that dragged his soul into the deep.

One day he took her hot, rough hand, looked her in the eyes, and begged.

"Madeleine. Let me stay with you forever."

Wearing a distracted smile, she peered into his lonely gray spirit. Her wild, vulgar heart would never belong to anyone—she felt immense satisfaction in that knowledge.

Soon after he realized he could not live without her, she left.

Memories can be sad, but sometimes they can also save you.
- Takayuki Ikkaku, Arisa Hosaka and Toshihiro Kawabata, *Animal Crossing: Wild World*

Sometimes my past seems so far away that it is not mine anymore. I look back at my life and barely recognize memories that were once part of me.

From the time I was a kid in my parents' house—completely engulfed in books—to the time I opened my heart to love, marriage, parenthood and other ruthless interactions with life, destiny carried me on paths I don't identify with anymore. You get hurt, you achieve fleeting happiness, you help people along the way, people help you, and through time you weave the tapestry of your existence.

I'm lucky because I had the great fortune of walking along side great people who helped me. My parents are the most important influence in my life, and though I don't have the patience or time to give them proper recognition, they possess a quiet understanding of their place in my heart.

While writing about them, my eyes well with tears—I have the urge to pick up the phone and talk to them, but once I'm on the phone I'm irritated and short-fused. Thusly, I repay their priceless gifts.

First Snow

While I looked at oranges standing in a line on top of my dresser, one fell and rolled next to my bed. In falling, the orange split in the way my dad splits them. It soaked the room with a faint citrus aroma. Then, there she was, standing and shivering in the cold room—a tiny orange fairy looking up at me. She giggled and flew around the room like a bumblebee. I followed her with my eyes, sometimes seeing her clearly, other times feeling only the air move gently to mark her passage. On the windowsill, she landed on the edge of my abandoned cup of milk.

"Want to see a miracle?"

I got up and approached the window. The floor was cold as I padded across it with bare feet. The white ice flowers once decorating the window are gone—the window is clean and clear. I hear buzzing from the air…the sky is very white and freckled with blue sparkles. The fairy landed in my open palm with translucent wings buzzing like a dragonfly. More and more glowing flakes fill the air.

Snow.

It's like this: the snow is blue—blue is the first snow. The first flakes are blue and fall gently with a buzzing, humming sound like a cloud of bees. The ground is blue. The trees are blue. The fence, covered in a soft blanket, is blue. Later I see flakes of mixed colors—blue-blue and blue-white. And then white-blue, increasingly white. White-white stars fall from the sky.

"Snow."

I opened the window and the fairy flew out. She became one with starry snowflakes—I could not tell them apart.

"My little princess," said my mother, "your feet are frozen, you slept without a cover."

"Come on! Get up! Let's see how our courtyard changed overnight."

Mom took my little hand and walked to the window to see the snow-covered yard. She does not know—but I know everything. She does not know that I talked to the orange fairy and saw the beginning of the season's first snow.

The house smelled like marmalade.

Mom gathered the oranges from the top of my dresser, sliced them and simmered their flesh in a big pot until the house smelled like a fairy tale.

The next year, I asked my father to open all the oranges before the first snow so I could see the fairy.

Anything I asked politely, he could not deny.

Oh, how I wanted to see the orange fairy and the first blue snow of winter.

I have no choice but to start all of my tales with *once upon a time...,* which is fair warning about their fictional fabric.

Believe what you wish—there are many on this face of our earth embracing events taken from books or television—trying to relive them in their backyards, streets, or schools. Full of themselves—swearing up and down that any story, however unlikely, could or did happen in their village.

Hey, kids, wake up…a story's a story, let's not confuse them with real events from our everyday lives.

We don't cloak our accounts in secrecy; we are unselfish and generous with our stories.

You should know this—any attempt to reposition this account into real life will make you look silly and the subject of ridicule and humiliation. I advise you to reconcile with the thought that luck finally came—but only on the heads of children on my street. We, and we only, participated in the tale I'm preparing to tell.

Many years have passed since I was a little girl...now I suppose you'd consider me an eccentric, old, rich lady, but I clearly remember how it was.

They say I have a fertile imagination…

Or something like that.

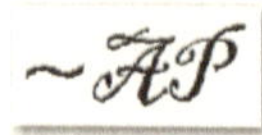

A Very Short and Silly Story about an Elephant called Raj Kapur

Once upon a time there was an elephant that lived as all elephants do except he was a unique kind of elephant. He did not live in India or Africa, but at the end of our suburban street.

Our elephant was recorded in the town's documents as Raj Kapur and he was larger than any other elephant in the world. Placed next to a normal elephant, the normal elephant would look like a baby.

If you looked down our street you could see Raj's back and bald head rising above the trees like a sad, barren hill. Anyone standing close to Raj, even the biggest and strongest man in the neighborhood, looked like a little boy. I am not even mentioning how a boy looked next to the giant elephant.

It was the greatest happiness for we kids to get close. Only a handful could reach the knuckle of his toe. And to climb up his hip? Goodness gracious. Firefighters would have to rescue you with a ladder, one of their long, long ones.

It was our luck that Raj did not mind the children who visited him; he was gentle and patient. Thus, when a kid whined and insisted on climbing to the top, Raj lowered his trunk to the asphalt and the kid simply climbed on. Grandfathers no longer appealed to firefighters for help. On top, you were high above everything—well above all the trees. At the end of the trunk raised heavenward, you realized how narrow our street and how small our neighborhood—when compared to rest of the city.

I want to emphasize that any boy or girl, once on top of the small world seen from the height of our elephant, became overcome by giddiness, glowing back to the heavens with the joy of being so small and yet raised so very high.

Ghost Words and other Echoes…

I 've had a vivid imagination for as long as I can remember; so vivid that the lines between reality and my thoughts and dreams were always blurry…at times, this scared the living daylights out of my parents. With fondness, I remember imaginary friends that lived in the palm of my hand—and the worried look on my mother's face as I carried on lengthy conversations with my little friends.

Reality is fragile…as we get older, we might hope to recapture a child's fantasy world, but we're terrified of acknowledging our limits—mapping the boundaries and borders of our existential fiber.

Fantasy is the exchange of imagined roles and real identities. Which displaces which? The end is the same. Illusions are a valuable framework for memories…when the imaginary world becomes real—tangible—you will never again enjoy a moment of pure silence or trust a smile.

Magic Orange Line

The child drew a line. So straight, clear and brightly orange that the line came alive. It moved its puny body, thrashed, and with a push—freed itself from the prison of white paper.

"Where do I begin?" the line asked while writhing in the air.

The little line wriggled—snaking and jumping in the air, leading first with one end and then with the other since it had no head.

The child laughed hysterically at the sight of the little orange line so confused and silly. Catching it between two fingers, she laid it back on the sheet of paper, and, with a blue pencil, drew a dot on one end. Happy now, the orange line, decorated with a blue dot, jumped again—this time confident of her looks.

"How beautiful is my head? I'm beautiful. Beautiful! Where's a mirror? I want to see myself in the mirror."

"Here it is."

The child produced a hand mirror from a drawer.

The line *was* beautiful.

"Yes. I am a very attractive line. But…I need a red ribbon to make me look finished. What do you say? So I might look more amazing, could you add a red silk bow around my skinny neck? Maybe with little green polka dots, that would be great. Faster, faster…give me my ribbon," said the impatient line.

The child picked up a red pencil and drew an elaborate bow. Then, with a green crayon, she added green splats. She couldn't stop laughing at how silly and alive the little orange line looked with a red bow bearing green spots. But the line acted conceited and selfish. It could not stop admiring its beauty—as if no other line as lovely existed. It turned and twisted in the little round mirror, bending and adjusting its neck ribbon and shaking its fragile little body in frenzy.

"Have you seen a head so pretty as mine?"

"Of course I have," the girl said, "anyone can have such a head."

The child was aggravated by the line's arrogant self-regard. The line was cute, but she drew it casually on a piece of paper—any other child could draw a line equally, if not more playfully, cute.

The child ruffled her shiny hair and raised it in a bunch to form a princess crown.

"What do you say? Do you love my head?"

"Mmm…yes," the line admitted with a weak voice. The child looked cute—the orange line was forced to admit the fact. "But I don't see a red bow with green polka dots around your neck."

The child looked feverishly through all the drawers where ribbons were kept, but could not find one anywhere.

How pretty she would look with a red ribbon.

She didn't care much for wearing silken bows but she wanted an antidote to the line's bossiness.

The line laughed at the child's consternation.

"Hahahaha!"

In a magic moment of perception, the child had an idea. She picked up an eraser. With bitter tears streaming down her cheeks, she erased the obnoxious line. Soon the paper was white and pristine. One blemish reminded her something was there before, but only she would know it was once a precocious, obnoxious green line.

* * * * *

The child grew up. One day she remembered the life of the little line and missed its high-pitched voice. She found an orange crayon and a white sheet of paper. After staring at the blank sheet for a moment, she drew a line…it remained lifeless on the white paper.

She tried another. And again, another.

She filled dozens of sheets with lines of many colors.

It was fruitless.

Each line was quiet and well behaved. After being murdered so coldly and cruelly, the naughty little line could not be resurrected.

November Breakup

November was cruel.

Outside the window, leaves were chased by the wind. From a leaden sky, hissing rain poured on skeletal oaks. The landscape was limned with a glossy-wet glow shed by an enslaved sun. He had no idea what time it was—if he should hurry, if he was still young or had grown old or was simply experiencing a twilight dream.

He lay in bed staring at the white ceiling—a white that was not so white—patched with gray dust and cobwebs. A burst of rain cast against the window broke the monotony. The room smelled of a young woman. Deodorant, hand cream, shampoo.

"I quit you."

"Just like that?"

"Yes, just like that."

She pulled a travel bag from the closet and crammed it full. A towel—with chubby, hand-stitched tomcat—a red-and-white cotton bathrobe and four books she could not part with. Hurrying, as if afraid he'd talk her into staying.

"It makes no sense," he said.

"Why?"

"It makes no sense and that's all. Like before, you'll get cold at the bus stop and come back shivering."

"Not this time."

He sensed the decision in her trembling voice.

This's what two years together means: knowing where and when you can be certain.

Over his head, her stuffed bear rested on a shelf. He never liked the bear—it had an enormous head and spooked him at night when the streetlight fell on it. She stretched to grab it—he tried to catch her in his arms…to kiss her? Stumbling, she fell on him—apologizing and springing up immediately.

She was ready—all dressed. The travel bag was closed and latched. Standing at the door, instead of looking at him, her gaze took in the furniture—window, floor lamp and television set—and the door going to the kitchen.

She pulled keys from her purse and set them on the table.

"Goodbye," she said.

Was she talking to him or the lamp?

"Goodbye," he said back to her.

He watched her slip through the door and close it carefully—quietly—to avoid bothering the old lady across the hall.

He jumped up and pressed his face to the window overlooking the street.

She knows I'm here. She knows. She'll look back. One more look...one last time.

Pulling away from the stop, the bus made a screeching noise. It disappeared in autumn mist.

He sat down on the bed and looked around the room. His keys, his books, his clothes…no more thrown-around mother of pearl brushes, perfume bottles with narrow spouts or hangers suspended from random pieces of furniture.

He threw the windows open wide. The incoming air was dour—as if tainted by memory. Two years of a shared life echoing with cheerful laughter and infused with melodramatic tension and sorrow. Two years of her life, his life, the ancient neighbor's life, the bed's life and the off-white ceiling's life.

It was hard to accept what he was already accepting.

Spasms in his chest…leaking eyes, stinging.

The room was deserted—cold and remote. He slammed the windows closed. Then, wrapped in her abandoned blanket, he fell into bed.

Later, with an empty soul, he got up, got dressed and left the room.

Go in this direction, then that...now I know what time it is. I see the green numbers flashing on the car display.

November—maybe the last one ever—the start or end of autumn, depending on how you care to look at it.

He stood at the bus stop, but waved for the buses to pass by. Finally, he gave up. Shivering, he walked back to his empty home.

Don’t Mind the Naked Man on the Couch—Chapter Six

There is no such thing as truth in a lover’s oath.
- Plato

For Matilda, youth was a tentative dance with ideas. She took little comfort from God and his promise of a happy afterlife—not reaching this conclusion through a dramatic, traumatic process, but in a gradual drift from faith. A void yearns to be filled…she buried her head in books.

When people turned their conversation from the ethereal to the practical, they talked about men—they spoke with admiration about bastards who gamed the system. In school, nearly everyone loved the new teacher…a drunken swindler and heavy-smoker with a promiscuous prick. Vlad was his name. The Impaler, the girls called him. A minor-grade scoundrel compared to Saul, but not for want of trying. He scoffed because the books she read were outside of the school's assigned, approved list.

"Messed-up books for a messed-up girl," he said.

He recited their titles with disgust and shook their pages with a gleeful fever—as if he expected pornographic photos to fall out.

"So, what *is* sin," he mocked, "are we talking about the Decalogue? Do not steal; do not lie. Are we exiled from Eden because of the original sin? Why does God punish those who defy him? Without us, He'd be bored."

Matilda knew about the seven *capital* sins: envy, immodesty, debauchery, desire, anger, laziness and adultery. She found it fun and interesting to see how these offenses manifested from one individual to another. The *easy* girl with the short skirt. The football player always ready to bloody his knuckles. The glib-tongued teacher with an irresistible, persuasive charm.

Other thoughts occupied her mind. There was a story she'd heard when she was a little girl—about a Dickensian shrew said to cut the cat's tail because it was too long and kept the door open too long in the winter. The story made her laugh…was it the stupidest thing she'd ever heard?

Where does God live?

Where is heaven and hell?

However, more importantly…where do celestial stars like Sirius and Vega fit in the cosmic picture?

In Dostoyevsky, a character believed God had a beard and lived in the sky. Another questioned in an analytical way the very concept of heaven and hell and ridiculed him. Dostoyevsky died in 1881, so, about the afterlife, he now knows what we do not.

The pitchforks Satan uses to keep order in Hell had to come from somewhere.

Where? Where did the wood come from and who cast the iron? If Hell is no place on earth, where could pitchforks come from?

The conundrum wedged in her consciousness when she read a line from Plato.

If death is the end of everything, then bastards and criminals are the winners.

This grasp on spirituality sent her mother into a state of panic mixed with open concern and sadness. Oddly, having never been fanatically religious before, Matilda's mother experienced an infatuation with sanctimony…perhaps the result of her own approaching mortality. She insisted Matilda spend time reflecting on her transgressions and set out on the road to redemption.

She was barely eighteen.

"What do you mean you don't believe the soul is immortal?" the priest said.

The chapel walls were covered with pictures meant to inspire pious sadness and spiritual calm…the stereotypical austerity of a mountain monastery.

"I just don't think it's so, Father."

"Oh, you've been spoiled. It happens. When you're older, you'll remember God and pray."

She wanted to swear an oath.

No, that will not happen.

The priest was not a fanatic…not with the idea of divinity, or with other ideas.

“That may come to be, Father,” she said with kindness.

Some people are anxious—tormented like the Dostoyevsky character—thinking God does not exist and therefore everything is allowed.

Matilda did not share this torment.

Instead, she felt a hidden jubilation.

Because she was free.

Don't Mind the Naked Man on the Couch—Chapter Seven

In art school, when Matilda was a girl holding onto grand illusions of paradise, there were foreshadows of the woman she'd later become. Step-by-step and every day, she tread a path into the unknown. Three years filled with steps, all through her college years. Like a sensuous, passionate tango—two steps forward, one back.

How many steps could she now take back in time?

Most people of her age were uninterested in philosophy or culture. What they did learn by rote was unassimilated. It was hard for Matilda to understand…if she were to idealize the situation she'd say they followed Rousseau's principle and remained natural, in a primal, unaltered form.

Culture abides pride.

By being primal and untouched by insight, they maintained the youthful beauty of their bodies.

"It could be read as a step towards virtue, as when Hamlet tells his sinful mother to fight the urge to go to the King's bed, even if the carnal desires cannot be cleansed from her mind."

In the victory of afterglow, Saul waxed philosophical as if deep thoughts could obscure sin. It was an intoxication she craved and clung to. Living for the moment, she poured herself into Saul's life and wrapped elaborate coils of vaporous chains around his heart.

Because she was a student borrowing master keys of the inner sanctum of the teacher's world, she was lonely and alienated when associating with her schoolmates. Like a tone-deaf sociologist, she studied her classmates' laid-back camaraderie.

One day, someone approached, grabbed her by her shoulders and whispered in her ear.

"Give up books...you know what Goethe said, one looks in the books and two into life..."

This encounter led to an invitation to a bodega called *Mother of the Injured*; a dark, small room obscured by the black smoke of many cigarettes. The proprietor, their mother of injured, oversaw the drinking. Fat and bearing an intense look, she apparently had strong feelings about her patrons.

Matilda wondered if they were indeed hurt…damaged beyond repair. She looked around. A woman screamed something intended to be a song. Everyone else spoke with loud voices over the blaring.

"Why is this place called *Mother of the Injured*?"

"No one knows. Mom comes here at night to hide from a man who steals her money."

Matilda removed her elegant autumn-brown and green overcoat and placed it on the backrest of her chair. She sat with a timid smile radiating from her delicate, oblong face. Her eyes were alive with the curiosity of the moment. With a magical smile fueled by cheap wine, her eyes grew lustrous and inquisitive…she let herself be carried away by the infectious spirit of the party.

It was pleasant and comforting to talk to people her age. She spoke, of course, not of philosophy, but about ordinary things—the tangible anchored in concrete. What was curious for her was that they did not converse with subtle claims for intellectuality like Saul's friends. Their thoughts were expressed with clarity and purity—unadulterated by over-analysis.

Later, she slipped through the dimensions of her disparate reality over-and-over—happily joining her classmates, then returning effortlessly to Saul's cerebral rabbit hole.

Her universe and time were made of ice with a diamond's perfect surface.

With her skin now soft and slack, her black hair was increasingly gray…as if winters nested in it. She dreamed what she lived and lived what she dreamed, with no escape or exit—sliding through dark tunnels looking for light.

The pace drifted at times, with her timid soul returning to what it was a long time ago. And sometimes, late at night, her skin remembered Saul's caress and came alive.

Bring Back our Mailman

Overnight, the mailman was given his termination notice. We don't know why and neither does the mailman. He was summoned to the Human Resources department through interoffice snail mail (ironic but we will leave it unexplored for now) and was told he no longer had a job.

With a beautiful family, grown children and a house purchased with the rewards of many years of quiet resentment, sweat and millions of steps on the same roads leading nowhere, he was happy with himself and his life.

He was never late to the job, never called in sick, and was well-regarded by his boss…only a few months away from retirement after forty-five years of honorable service without losing a letter. Sometimes even delivering the same letter twice.

What? Delivering a letter twice?

He believed delivering good news a second time would bring forth the same joyful reception. So he'd wait and read the letter with the recipient (often an unexpected situation for the host) and be overcome with joy if the letter's news was cheerful. He'd make up a silly reason for snagging the letter back from the puzzled receiver to come back the next day to deliver, with jolly flourish, the same envelope one more time.

There was never a formal complaint.

Now and then bad news had to be delivered. He'd tear the letter in half or quarters and deliver only part…to hurt less, he told the surprised recipient.

Over time, people learned their mailman's quirks and no one protested. They embraced him as a skewed dimension of their lives. His tacit love protected, sheltered, and embraced them. He was someone to share joy or misfortune with.

They learned how good news was separated from bad news. The former taken with reckless joy, while the dismal latter was endured with great stoicism.

Gradually, fewer letters came—it was as if people forgot the art of letter writing. After thinking things through, the mailman decided to write the letters and telegrams himself.

In a short time the numbers of healthy, happy children and grandchildren increased…incurable patients miraculously recovered and fewer tears were shed at funerals. Mediocre students received high marks while prosperity and wealth grew in the hard-working neighborhood.

Everybody was happy.

Until one day…when the community began giving him long, strange glances.

At first, sad shakes of heads…followed by concerned looks.

Day and night, winter and summer and regardless of inclement weather…good and bad news filtered into every house on every block through cables and airwaves and other digital marvels. Good and evil tidings flowed through walls like ghosts.

Through television, nonstop news programs found its audience every day. Salaries and pensions trickled into bank accounts without mailed letters.

The mailman became unnecessary.

On the street, they greeted him as they would a pleasant memory from long ago…as a relic of times past.

Then the disaster began. People started dying. Today one, tomorrow another, and no one knew why. Some spoke of a secret virus…a strange and unknown disease coming from nowhere.

Research and investigative effort led nowhere.

Wireless phone chatter exacerbated the disturbance. Everyone felt eerie and anxious without reason or explanation. When a full day passed and nobody received any news, the anxious tapped their monitors with shaking hands. Nothing. Everything was in vain.

A car hit a power pole on Main Street and the power was out throughout their neighborhood. They lamented and asked the heavens.

"How is this possible? In what kind of world do we live? The mailman came every day…even when he was sick."

The electricity came back but the joy was short-lived. News was sent a million times a day but there was no one to discuss it with, to explore subjects and analyze themes—to deliberately exaggerate and sow envy between neighbors.

The cold, impersonal electronic screen displayed good and bad news without judgment. Details about cardiovascular incidents, car breakdowns and distant relatives' deaths were discharged in a cold, blunt manner. Lab results from hospitals sent shivers up people's spines because no one softened the blow. People were left alone with faceless strangers at the end of wires and cables who gradually became their enemies and cold-blooded executioners.

By now, everyone was desperate. The electronic delivery of letters and news did not require gratuities or a glass of wine…did not ask about rheumatism, gout, weather, or errant children. It was mutually decided this kind of life was not for them. They said *no* to modern times and gathered signatures on a petition to ask for their mailman back…the mailman they happily tipped a buck or two for a beer. Or two.

"Please bring him back," they said, "at double-salary if that's what it takes."

They pleaded for their mailman and no other...their omnipotent friend who knew so well how to properly deliver a letter. No one answered.

As word has it—the e-mail was deleted.

The Artist Fisherman

If you saw someone carrying a fishing pole and bearing a backpack on his back, a straw hat on his head and rubber boots on his feet, you'd be willing to bet he was a fisherman. You'd be dead wrong and lose this bet in the case of the artist fisherman.

Our character could hardly care less about fish. Yes, the unruffled waters of the lake at the edge of town created a magnetic attraction in him—a smooth surface for his thoughts.

His wife knew there would be no fish for dinner—she attacked the absurdity of her man's behavior.

"What kind of mind guides you? Why do spend so much time at the bog if you do not catch fish? Why do you spend so much money on fancy fishing poles and gear cluttering my closet?"

The man gave his wife a long, puzzled look.

How could she not see the substance of his weekly departures?

"Dear," he said while trying to master annoyance, "I do not wish to catch fish. I throw out the line to get past the surface of my thoughts—thoughts that swim on the marshy bottom of my conscience."

The woman shrugged.

I had to marry an artist...were there no engineers or teachers available?

She walked to her freezer and pulled out a big fish, to be ready when the fisher of thoughts came back with the red sun behind him—without a spectacular catch.

Invariably, after sailing his waters, the artist fisherman came home bearing a broad smile after many hours spent in the shade of a shaggy willow pulling thought after thought from the water. The man felt weightless—free of burdens and fears—as if his mind was cleansed by an endless rain.

To perfect the paradoxical illusion, he learned all the expert tricks of fishing. Assuming he ever tried fishing for real, he would have an excellent chance of catching many. Instead, he did not step over the self-imposed barrier. While standing on lakeshore, original thoughts were all he was after.

Back home, with a smile riding his lips, he would kiss his woman's cheek, take a cup of brandy and disappear into his office.

There, hunched over a laptop computer, he would strip bloody splatters of sentences and gory, glistening words from fresh-caught thoughts.

An Absurd Scenario for Artists

Writers, painters, musicians, people of all arts and experts in varied sciences gathered in front of the data-printing warehouse.

Barely breathing in their excitement—some held flash drives, some CDs—all waited to print their creations, visions and dreams on a silicon-embalmed sheet.

The artists patiently waited in line.

Most secretly harbored inner desires to transform the linear parameters they grew up with into enduring multidimensional binary masterpieces.

The painter needed a new chip for converting his paintings…something that would bring his drab colors to life and impress his audience. Or better, take his admirers by surprise. He also wanted a higher resolution for his images.

The writer wanted two chips with extraordinary binary power...so powerful that his poem-writing program would merge with his prose-writing program to cross the pedestrian and produce immortal works. He also wished for higher resolution for his cover, maybe a 32-bit color unit, and wait…additional fonts to enhance his text.

The composer wanted to add twenty-four channels to his sound card…the rocker, to add a further ten decibels to the current hundred to create blusterous and invasive echoes and harmonies.

Policemen also waited. Next to them was parked an armored car filled with soldiers. The police came to transfer money from the United State Bank to the Ministry of Social Protection. The funds were needed to finance the Criticism and Negative Response Elimination project.

In fact, they were at the point of exchanging the money for their own chip. The new digital system gave them the opportunity to intercept brain waves emitted by an offender. For example, someone rejecting a new art project. The booing rebel would be in a stumbling state of confusion until the police could arrest him.

Also waiting was the General. He was tasked to replace a defective chip in a nuclear bomb that stubbornly refused to explode during a field test.

The data compiler loaded the software waiting in the data warehouse storage and turned it into a binary script. An electronic robot with laser eyes pushed a button to print each sheet of silicon, which then rolled out on a conveyer.

The smell of freshly-printed silicon gave the General a deep feeling of satisfaction. The sight of freshly packaged chips produced a satisfied smile on his barren face.

To him, the situation did not seem absurd at all.

Adina Pelle

Don't Mind the Naked Man on the Couch—Chapter Eight

Saul's tone was casual. His legs were spread and his arms were stretched across the back of the couch as if completely unaware of his nudity.

"Remember art school?"

Matilda was deep in thought…accompanied by past ghosts and too preoccupied to be scared or frustrated by Saul's naked, cocky presence. His self-confident manhood was an obsession his ego orbited around. His stories were infused with a feral force—indecent and vulgar. People enjoyed the guilty pleasure of his dirty jokes. Early in their relationship, Matilda was his best audience.

For example, the story of the Seventh Day Adventist woman having an affair. She asked her lover to cover his prick, as if not seeing it would absolve her of sin…he ended up wearing a sheet with a carefully-positioned hole. The story was ridiculously plebeian, but amused Matilda back then—she could not hide a sleepy grin even now.

"I was mad and delusional in art school," she said in answer to his question.

Of course she remembered.

Saul loved to hear himself speak.

Saul waxed philosophical as if deep thoughts, like the Adventist's sheet, could obscure sin. His eerie presence dissipated as she dived into her pool of memories. Living for the moment in those days, she poured herself into Saul's life and wrapped elaborate coils of vaporous chains around his heart—kissing him without hurry, but with unexpected passion.

Like Magellan, he explored her privacy—as a green-eyed ogre, he consumed her innocence. Her naked body, unmarked by time and unravaged by maturity, was both battleground and prize.

Don't Mind the Naked Man on the Couch—Chapter Nine

What is life?
What isn't?

Life is everything, and the way it's lived can be hypnotizing. The spirit is in the center; its purpose is to fight to save itself. Some say: only after abandoning a search for peace and happiness can you finally experience it. In reality, happiness as well as misfortune follows us wherever we go…in any of life's caves or burrows.

She saw Louise one night at *Mother of the Invalids*—one of many prostitutes loitering in the stale, smoky room before launching into the night to sell themselves in dark alleys.

No man came to them to fall in love with the exposed merchandise...each purchased a service according to the size of their wallet. With analytical dispassion, Matilda watched Louise every night…unclear on the difference between purchase and conquest. Just as art is not measured by eternal, inherent truths, but through subtle effects of light and shadow, was the game between prostitute and client. Those paying replaced several minutes of darkness with artificial light.

Every night Louise drank moss-green absinthe before dipping into the night. It was strikingly obvious—a woman like her entertained no illusions.

Love never survives the cutthroat struggle with convenience...nothing survives except hope; truth does not yield to deceit.

There was an uncomfortable parallel between Louise's reality and Matilda's—misguided morality was a stain on both women's consciences. Louise performed a clumsy amputation of memory to evade pain. Her conclusion? That holiness was not an option. Matilda lived in a suspended, dizzying ambiguity searching for her place in the odd stream of life.

Louise was young and beautiful. She had marvelous legs visible between fur coat and black boots. Her face was beautiful too—with eyes bearing long lashes blinking against cigarette smoke.

There are beautiful faces and that's all there is about them…accidents of nature. However, a face bursting with inner light, full of a lifetime of thoughts and emotions, with eyes drawing you in, the triumph of a cheek with beaming white skin and a mouth which could not stay closed because of excitement within, a relish for life and imbedded depravity—in such a face, beauty abided.

Louise walked every night after sunset and her dose of absinth through a secret space peripheral to fictional, negotiated love. When thrown in the middle of a war of unequals, human nature is weak and helpless. Matilda knew this better than anyone. It was curious how the rental of the body was less harmful than the sellout of ideas and spirit through corrupted thinking.

Each of us lives the lie we deserve.

Louise walked with death in her purse. As a stygian bargain, she carried a container of sleeping pills.

"I think old age is a mess anyway. I will die young," she told Matilda one day before disappearing.

Maybe she used her death tube or moved to the country and had kids. One's life can be remastered.

Except when you are foreign to your soul.

They say death is nature's simplest truth—people make it sound scary. Louise was attracted to melancholy, as if nostalgic for a return to peace.

Like lying in a field, with eyes glued to a star-studded sky until falling asleep.

In the mountains, our bus, like a creeping worm, slowly climbed the steep country road, shaking and threatening to dismantle itself with every bumpy rut.

I was twelve-years-old...when you're twelve, any road to the unknown is always the first road...the only magical way of leaving childhood behind. I watched the forested hills above the road—ghostly tree trunks guarded an azure sky. White smoke climbed the sky like snow in reverse—rising snow sucked into clouds.

With an infernal noise, our old bus stopped in a valley between hills. Inside were twenty kids with mouths full of dust collected during hours of riding over dirt roads with the windows open. In single-file, we exited. The others sat on logs. I was the only one who walked away—trying to see beyond the wall of smoke—beyond the mysterious fire burning from nothing. The smell of burnt wood—for me, was an olfactory bliss.

In the middle of the smoke, I saw a ghostly silhouette. A white shadow came toward me...my heart beat rapidly...loud in my ears...I wanted to yell. I wanted to run.

Before me stood a Gypsy woman, wearing overlapping skirts. Colorful, as if in bloom.

I wanted to ask what kept the fire alive but I was silenced by her eerie presence. Blood, sucked by my terrified heart, drained from my cheeks.

The Gypsy woman looked at me as if stealing secrets from my mind. I closed my eyes. For a moment before the chaperones found me, the world disappeared.

The road our bus climbed so many years ago is still there, hidden between smoke and sky. I never went back to see the Gypsy, but I've thought of her often.

And the fire?

It still burns in the pit of my belly.

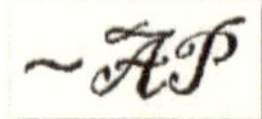

Gypsy

It was a day with crying clouds—gray skies and gray roads—when I started my march to nowhere. I remember her as if she's in front of my eyes—with eyes torn from dreams. Eyes the spectacular texture of onyx and a smile stripped from the majestic sphere of the sacred. The air weighed heavy with chanting.

She was—because I sipped her godly poison—an amalgam of surrealism; she wore my wonderful chimera of fear.

I proclaim it proudly: I read the formula in her red Gypsy dance. I read it in her lips and breasts and the dark places under arched arms and between protective thighs. Her peasant skirt flicked erratically in a pagan ballet. Spinning broken circles. Rotation changing as abruptly as it began. Thousands of colors, garish in the sun and pale in the shade.

So many faces in her skirt. She twirled and I saw another side and back to the other hidden side and hidden to the other, and the other side and other side—how many threads to bind, how many souls hidden in her skirt? How many times had I reassembled my life? I played at spinning dizzily into exhaustion.

Back then, I knew everything.

Dancing red and black and naked in the middle of the road.

There was no one else to take her message to the damned. I was the crying man, the weeping man, the sobbing man.

I found monsters and creatures buried in her memories and discovered her penetration by demons and angels. She unleashed and welcomed them—I knew my Gypsy was turned into an ordinary slut selling herself at the gates of heaven and hell. The flesh they bought, the answers they sought…in knowing, I never got the simple thing I wanted: a heart-felt smile.

Maybe We Will Meet Again

Sometimes, life is strange.

Nothing new here, but when you witness a true story, you automatically think…

Life can be odder than any movie.

This true story began some years ago. On a wonderful autumn day in the park, I met an old man. He was cheerful, smart and engaging—with a great talent at telling stories.

I sat on a bench looking at a mirror-like lake…watching the wind push fallen leaves floating like small ships.

"Do you mind?"

I heard a friendly voice coming from behind.

"No, please sit," I said.

The old man perched next to me on the bench.

"Of all the benches in the park," he said, "I chose this one. Whenever I come here, I sit on this bench; it's my favorite. From here I can see the whole lake…ducks and weeping willows stirred by the breeze."

"Yes," I said in reply while staring at willowy branches dancing in the wind.

"On this bench, I met her," the old man whispered before lapsing into silence. I turned my head to watch him carefully. In the sunset light, his eyes glowed with strange happiness. "You think I am too old to love," he added, "but love takes no account of age. I am physically old, yes, but I have a young heart. Only through experience and the accumulation of years can one learn a commitment to true love. Were you ever in love?"

"Well…"

He allowed me no time to complete my thought.

"What can elevate more than deep, pure love? When I see her, I flicker like a wind-teased flame. I stutter, I perspire…my throat dries like a fossil. I am thirsty, hungry and dizzy all at once. And that is only when I see her…when she talks to me? I feel love as I imagined it in my youth."

I looked at him. His eyes wandered across on the surface of the lake.

"She is younger, but this is no impediment. If only I was free...I am married and have two boys..."

Silence. Each immersed in their thoughts. I thought of asking him if he no longer loved his wife. It was as if he anticipated my question.

"Often, marriages are merely conveniences."

"What do you mean?" I asked.

Instead of answering, he got up and walked away.

"I hope to see you again," I called out to his retreating back.

* * * * *

We met again two years later in the busy hallway of the courthouse—as I finalized my divorce. We recognized each other and smiled. He was very well dressed.

"If you can, come to the park…you know the bench," he said.

I waited for the old man. It was an autumn day similar to the first time we met. The willow tree looked shaggy and mean, as if mad at the coming winter.

"Were you waiting long?"

Tearing my eyes from the weeping willows, I turned as the old man approached the bench.

"No, actually I do not even know exactly how much time has passed."

"In this park and on this on this bench, time flies," he said.

From a bag, he pulled a bottle of champagne and two plastic glasses.

"This day is big one for me. Unique. Today my divorce complete and I am happy. I'm free to marry the woman I love…the one true love of my life."

With careful and delicate movements he placed the glasses between us and opened the bottle.

"Let's drink to happiness and love. You're happy, right?"

"Yes, I am happy," I answered.

"Now, in old age, I want to know love. Do you condemn me?"

"No, I could not..." But again, I could not finish my sentence.

"All through youth," he said, "I had no one to give my love...tenderness, comfort, affection, immense love and understanding. Now I am alive because I have true love by my side."

He stopped talking and we drank from our plastic glasses. Ahead, the sun drowned in the lake. With fascination, I watched. Happiness was written on his face. His eyes were clear. Age, for some, is gift, not an impediment.

"Now I have to go."

To tease me, he hummed a tune while walking away from the bench.

After a time, I recognized it.

Maybe We Will Meet Again.

* * * * *

Several years later I walked through the park and saw the usual sad homeless people looking through garbage bins for dinner or abandoned treasures. Among the scavengers, an old man caught my attention. Wearing expensive but dirty clothes, he was clearly embarrassed by what he was doing.

My old friend.

I stopped to stare. He nodded in greeting.

"Yes, it's me, the happy man."

Pathetic. My old friend looked pathetic. All happiness was erased from his face.

His voice was barely a whisper. "If you are embarrassed, walk away."

All words were stuck in my throat. My eyes asked the question.

What happened?

"My love is dead," he said, "my great love and everything is dead."

"My condolences," I managed to say.

There was cold bitterness in his laugh.

"No, my wife and son are alive, that's not it. They're alive and happy. In me, love died, my big love and joy of life..."

I shook my head with the wonder of it. At the time, there was no understanding in me. But later, I knew.

Maybe We Will Meet Again.

Three Witches

Ahmet was reminded of a time when he was in a hut with a single, final coin in his pocket. The city broiled in overheated summer. He looked at deserted alleys where all shutters were closed; the city felt abandoned.

When you are a young artist, you move through life with fraudulent ease.

His walk was assaulted by the inescapable flame of the summer afternoon. He leaned against the wall of a building and fanned himself. Then, without hurry, walked again when the smell of crushed walnut leaves tickled his nostrils. He stopped and looked around with curiosity. No one was around…the streets were deserted. He was immersed in white, blinding, incandescent light and suffered the hot air moving over his body.

Slowly moving forward, with his head bent to avoid low-hanging branches, he found himself before a gate. There, hidden like a spy in the shade, was a young girl, dark and beautiful—wearing large gold coins as earrings. She smiled and spoke in a whisper.

"Come for the fortune tellers?"

Her smile was all mouth and eyes—he staggered as she pulled him into the yard. He hesitated after a few steps and stopped, as if forgetting something.

"You want to see the fortune tellers?" the girl asked again.

He could barely hear her quiet voice.

She looked deeply into his eyes, then took his hand and led him behind the gate to an olive-green cottage hidden behind lilac bushes. She opened the front door and pushed him forward. Ahmet entered the dark room; it was filled with a curious hue, as if the windows were made of blue-green glass filtering the bright sunlight. Sitting at a short-legged table with a steaming cup was an old woman watching him curiously, as if waiting for him to awaken.

"Who would you like to see today?" she asked. "Gypsy, Greek, and Jewish fortune tellers?"

"No," Ahmet raised his arms and shaped the words in the air. "I don't care for the Gypsies."

"Well then, Gypsy, Greek and Jewish witches," replied the old woman with severe disapproval "will be one gold coin." The old woman took a sip from her cup. "Are you a musician?"

"Not a common musician, I'm an artist," said Ahmet while feverishly exploring his pockets. He looked in each methodically, one by one. "For my sins I play the violin for anyone who pays but my ideal is pure art. I live for the soul."

When he found the coin, he handed it to the old lady.

"Take him to the villa," the old woman said.

Ahmet felt a hand touching his arm; he turned his head to see the girl who lured him at the gate.

Following her—intimidated—he heard the old woman speak one more time.

"Remember them all...Gypsy, Greek, and Jewish witches."

The street was awash with bright light.

"Where are we going?"

They approached a wooden gate.

"To the hut."

To hurry him, she grabbed his arm and pulled him along.

"I'm excited," he said, "but I don't know why."

"Do not drink anything they offer," she said before opening the shack's door and pushing him inside.

It was a room with hidden corners—dark because the shutters were closed. Blind, he walked forward…walking on thick, soft carpet. His heartbeat quickened—until he was afraid to move any further forward. His heart flooded with a sudden happiness, as if he was young again and Mara was his once more.

"Mara," he mumbled. "I have not thought about you in twenty years. You were my great love, the woman of my life."

He smelled a faint, exotic scent and heard someone clapping. As his eyes adjusted to the light, he saw the light increase in a mysterious way, as if curtains were drawn back slowly, very slowly, gradually letting the afternoon light in.

He blinked and three young girls appeared a few feet in front of him—clapping their hands, and laughing.

"So you have chosen," said one. "Gypsy, Greek, and Jewish witches."

"Let's see if you can guess which witch is which," said the second.

"See if you can tell which of us is the Gypsy," added the third.

Ahmet wondered if they thought he had no imagination to guess what a Gypsy looked like, especially with the young, beautiful, nearly naked girls right in front of him. He knew them as soon as he laid eyes on them. The very dark one, with black hair and brown eyes was, without doubt, the Gypsy. The second—wrapped in a pale-green veil and wearing golden shoes, with blond hair and skin white as a pearl, could only be the Greek woman. The third was Jewish—with a long, cherry-colored velvet blouse that left the shoulders and the tops of her breasts naked. She had bright red hair gathered and braided artistically on top of her head.

All three taunted him.

"Guess…which of us is the Gypsy."

Ahmet stretched an arm, pointed at the dark girl in front of him and spoke solemnly.

"Because all great artists are tested, even if only with a childish test like this, I'll answer. You—you are the Gypsy."

In the next moment, the girls holding his hands spun in circles, with him in the middle, shouting and singing, sounding as if their voices came from very far away.

"You didn't guess correctly."

Looking around in wonder, he heard them as if in a dream. It seemed like a different room, though he recognized the armchairs, sofa, and mirrors.

He felt fatigued and wobbly—under a spell. His beating heart raced with a dizzying speed and his body shivered.

"When I was in love with Mara," he whispered, "we dreamed of taking a trip to Greece."

"You were a fool," the dark girl interrupted. "Don't dream—live and love only for real."

"We were young…I was twenty and she was not yet eighteen."

The dark girl grabbed his hand and whispered urgently.

"Come with me."

She pulled him behind a lace-draped mirror and he found himself in a different room with scattered pillows, wooden chests and a floor covered with carpets. The walls were covered with large and small mirrors cut into strange shapes.

"Guess with care, artist," hissed the red-haired girl, "and you'll see how much fun life can be."

"Who's the Gypsy? Who's the Gypsy? Who's the Gypsy?" asked all three at once, surrounding him and spinning him in a teasing game.

"What's the matter?" inquired the red-haired girl. "Why can't you guess?"

"He remembered something lost in the past," said the Greek woman.

The dark girl he picked as the Gypsy took a few steps forward and smiled.

"I am Jewish," she said.

"Ah!" exclaimed Ahmet.

He hit his confounded forehead with his palm.

She held something faraway in her eyes and wore a veil, like a shy virgin of the Old Testament. The girl with red hair burst into laughter.

"Maybe you think I'm scared," he said. He tried hard to appear in control. "I chose you because I felt sorry for you. That's the truth. I said to myself 'Ahmet, with girls like these you must think…pretend to be fooled...let them think you don't know that some Gypsies have red hair.'"

The blonde laughed.

He realized he was alone in the dark room.

"Where are you?" he shouted. Fear of being alone filled him to overflowing.

"It was Mara," he said with a lonely voice filled with desperation. "She was my beautiful Gypsy."

There was no one around to hear him say he was sorry.

Dream Conversation with Myself

With frail hands clutching a tiny cluster of colorful wildflowers, she wore a subtle smile disclosed only at the corners of her mouth. Approaching slowly and timidly…swinging rubbery arms with every step. At first, she said nothing while toddling on bare feet—stepping carefully on fine layers of dust parched by an angry sun.

Like a hiding snake, her presence wrapped around my mind—strangling empty spaces.

Sinuous coils of braided locks lay on her shoulders—she looked unkempt and ghostly with milky white skin and blue eyes like reflections in the night. Her fleshy lips were poached by summer's boiling cauldron. A sharpened chin gave her an old, tired look. I know her—I have known her all my life. But, I never thought to stop and talk to her.

Until now.

"Who are you? How should I call you?"

"Why think to name someone who does not exist?"

"I like to name everyone and everything. Even little dream girls."

This was wholly and completely true. Compulsively true.

I smiled with satisfaction because of my perfect answer.

"Let me ask you, then," she chirped with unconscious nonchalance, "do dreams crumble? What happens to people who live in a dream that's later destroyed?"

"I compare dead dreams with autumn leaves—they persist for a time, but fade and crumble under the influence of the seasons. An ambitious dream will not make compromises needed for survival."

She must have not liked my words.

"People have critical periods. If they pass those events, they survive to tell stories to their grandchildren."

"True enough," I said, "but you want to tell your grandchildren a perfect story…ideal and without blemish."

"By the way…" she looked directly into my eyes, as if in a mirror. "What happened to me? What's my story?"

"You died. As a child, you fought death, but lost the battle. Your story is legendary; a myth that walks beyond reality. You changed the world in unimaginable ways before fading away."

"Being dead, how could I change the world?"

"You were part and parcel of perfection." My eyes gazed past her. "Perfection has no place on this earth, so it's often destroyed. But no one can touch you—you are beyond this world."

"If you lived for perfection, you should now be dead, like me," she argued, "maybe that's why you talk with me now."

"You live through me…through my thoughts."

"Then you'll tell and retell my story?"

I heard the challenge in her voice.

"No one will listen." I could not hold back my anger. "With each their own—living and dead. I had childhood dreams of myth and perfection I will not build on now. You, you…little goddess." I teetered on the edge of life's mad balustrade. "The world was smaller when I knew you well."

With vague mockery in her eyes, she bent her head forward and made faint patterns in the dust with her toes.

"Could you take steps forward to leave despair behind?" I did not have time to answer before she continued her inquisition. "It's peculiar? Strange to see me here and now?"

"Nothing surprises me."

"Don't try to lie to me," she said calmly. "You were surprised to see me again." Satisfaction is evident on her face. My sadness troubles her—she changes her tone. "I never met anybody so sneaky and ruthless, but at the same time so beautiful."

An odd way to win my sympathy.

"You give me pep talks now?" I ask with polite sarcasm, as a teacher would react to a student asking an impertinent question.

Shaking her head, she did not answer; her world disappeared when I opened my eyes. Blinding light streamed through imperfectly fitted window shades. Fantasies and dreams are valuable assets to one's memory, but if they are too real, they leave no room for happiness.

Noting my reflection in the window, I had a sad realization. I look like my father when someone cheated him: stiff, stuffy and authoritarian. There was nothing innocent and forgiving in my eyes.

As a child, I thought big, specific dreams could change my destiny and that my guardian angel would always look out for me.

A speckle of dust floated in the sunlight. I reached out my hand and captured it.

Don't Mind the Naked Man on the Couch—Epilogue

The backward trip through her life, as she remembered it, was induced by the green-eyed, dream-man-ogre. Despite the many trials, Matilda was thrilled by gems of pleasure embedded in the ruins of her history. She earned the right to draw any conclusion from her past experiences, but released her conscience by looking back and accepting all suffering, laughter, dreams and love.

Overall, the price was worthy of the reward.

The eternal hourglass of existence was turned over.

Lately, she liked walking free—without thought or destination…especially without dreaming, because in a conscious state she missed things. Thus, a great joy grew within. She walked while hearing, seeing, and smelling, with a quiet surprise from time to time, like chuckling at the sight of a random man skipping cracks on a sidewalk.

Under the morning sun, the city was a projection of her state of mind—a celebration of victory over ups and downs; triumph over lethargy left over from the events of her life. Without a conscious plan, she'd conquered unassailable territory. Now, years later, she reclaimed lost freedom.

In a summer dress she stood by David and listened to the reedy voice of the man before them.

"And now, by the power vested in me…I pronounce you…"

Her soul spread wings like a butterfly. On this magical day, the smell of meadow, garden—with fields alive with grass—penetrated King David's manly defenses. Her radiated luster was his to revel in; the images of this miraculous day glittered like morning dew on a flower. Her smile, like biblical seed in fortuitous soil, sprouted in David's heart and erased all residue of life's drama. His heart throbbed with nature's rhythm—rock solid and steady.

Matilda was the woman David imagined his whole life. As if fresh from paradise—she was luminous with lingering foreignness of accent and attitude. The smell of freshly-ironed cotton drifted over the aroma of almonds.

"You may now kiss the bride."

The sweet, wet softness of her mouth—soft and intimate like a rose.

Strobe-lit moments of intensity mixed with passionate purity…he loved everything that was wrong with her—her constant connubial struggle and other investments in wisdom. She looked over assembled friends and family—seeking inspiration.

"It's the Zen conundrum again. Stars, galaxies, what's the point? Everyone is hooked into everyone else, whether a little proton or a galaxy, a yin or a yang."

As she talked, he smiled—imagining meadows around her swarming with bees and birds and butterflies, where he could sleep and dream and contemplate the sky and clouds—to wake at sunset to prove one way or another if she was really the prodigal woman returning to her garden.

The myth of happiness through love was a continual contradictory theme, like dying and emerging into perpetual life. Her steps would be followed countless times by many others.

One truth stood out forever.

Without love, there is nothing.

In a far corner of her mind, there was still a naked man on the couch—Saul, the green-eyed ogre. Vrjen leaned in the doorway—and in the kitchen, someone rattled dishes.

"We're all naked in the spotlight of truth," Saul said.

She stood with arms and legs spread in supplication…as if ready to be nailed to an imaginary cross. His greedy eyes flicked over soft, secret curves.

"And now it's time for you to go," she said. "All of you."

Saul smiled with cold cruelty. "I won't be cast aside so easily."

Matilda laughed.

"You're already gone," she said.

And he was. They all were. Only the faint scent of his cigar remained. She walked to the bedroom and crawled under the covers next to David.

"What?" he said—a groggy whisper.

"Go back to sleep," she said.

www.ingramcontent.com/pod-product-compliance
Lightning Source LLC
Chambersburg PA
CBHW030338310726
48979CB00001B/81

9780975431467